The Heart of the Hydra

A novel by
A. Mangina

FLUKY FICTION
Newport, ME

Legal Shib'

This book is a work of fiction. Names, characters, places, and incidents are either products of the author's imagination or are used fictitiously. Any resemblance to actual persons, living or dead, or actual events is purely coincidental.

www.flukyfiction.com

A special thank-you to Margaux Kreder and Michaela Martell: the brave first readers.

*For Matt Stone and Trey Parker.
Sorry.*

Chapter 1

The Air Freshener of Life

Maybe moving was a hasty decision. I can't help but wonder whether I was being, perhaps, just a tad dramatic. Yes, the need for change was undeniable, but there are other ways of satisfying that desire. You know — a new hair color, a fresh coat of paint on the bedroom walls, a small, cuddly pet of some sort — but a change in *physical location*? That's a big deal. It's like saying, "Oh, this coffee is a little bitter; let me sweeten it up," and then pouring the **ENTIRE BAG** of sugar into the mug. Not that all-natural raw cane sugar, either: the most granulated sugar in existence. The stuff diabetes is made of. I should have thought this thing through. Or, I should've at least thought about it for a *little* longer than a week's time. Aren't you supposed to approach this type of shit a little bit at a time? Do you want to starve, or get raped?

Alright, Harper, now you're being dramatic. What's worse, you are internally dialogue-ing with yourself in the third-person. I think that might be a sign of insanity in itself. South Harbor is the runt of the East Coast cities with a population of only 60,000 people. It is barely a city. This you know for a fact because you pillaged the Internet of any and all information on this place before you packed up your first pair of panties. It's not like you moved to New York where there are literally millions of people coexisting (just over 8 million, according to the most recent census). The city dwellers here are more interested in getting their favorite fedora washed and publicly displaying their beer or seafood snobbery than forcing themselves into any of your orifices. You could only be so lucky...

And money? Um, you have been eating Chunky Soup for two months now. Why worry about starvation when the process has already begun? Would you worry about leaving a jug of milk on the counter when it's a week past its expiration date? You know it's clumped up beyond help at this point, so why bother worrying about it?

Slowly, I take a damp, shaky breath and drop my focus back to the cardboard box I've been steadying myself with. The sides look mashed and wilted like soggy bread once my hands leave their safety. I guess I'm tenser than I'd expected. No anxiety or second thoughts had crept into my mind during the car ride up here. There was the typical late-night-drive anxiety in the beginning of my evacuation since I had to flee in the middle of the night to avoid waking up my parents, but that was to be expected.

Questions and second-guessing were the last things that I needed. I needed to get out. Fast. I think my parents knew that I wasn't dealing with my circumstances well, but like most people — including myself, I think they were unsure of how to help.

The drive was horribly long. And horribly lonely. It was the longest drive I've been on by myself, and it was the longest eight hours of my life. Thank Christ that Vlad, my rusty piece-of-shit Impala, is equipped with a CD player. Otherwise, I wouldn't have been able to drown out the memories of this last month with my eardrum shattering renditions of my progressive rock collection. Somehow, I managed to only stop for gas once. I rolled onto the broken pavement of my apartment's driveway just as the gas light came on and as the sun peaked over the bay behind me. I'm not sure if this was divine intervention or the universe's way of attempting to add some balance to the heaping pile of garbage that has been dealt to me.

The warm rays of sunlight shining upon the front door of the apartment building would have been beautiful. That is, had the building not been dilapidated. I did appreciate the juxtaposition, though. I hadn't expected much, especially since the landlord accepted the signed lease and check I'd sent him after one phone conversation. I'll admit that I was initially a little worried that maybe he was just some drug addict posting fake ads on Craigslist and that said apartment did not even exist. As soon as I saw the key hidden in the agreed upon location (under the doormat — high security place, man), my stomach settled.

Walking through the door of my shitty (but freshly fumigated — what a perk) apartment didn't cause me to bat an eye, but unpacking has finally made this a reality. There's a sense of finality to the unpacking process. Before the boxes are cut open and gutted, there is still the possibility of hefting them right back into the car and speeding back up that interstate. The boxes are open. There's no turning back now. I mean, think about how senseless it would be to take the innards out of a box only to shove them right back in moments later? That's time that could be spent taking a bath, peeling off all my hangnails, or searching for funny Internet memes.

You're doing it again: using jokes as a shield from potentially exasperating ideas. This is one of the reasons why you left in the first place. Humor, like Febreeze, isn't going to make your shit stink less. All you're doing is covering it up with the artificial scent of flowers, but that stink will still seep through, and that freshness always fades away at some point. Besides, girls aren't funny.

Girls aren't funny.

This has been the anthem of my existence because God forbid a girl *tries* to be funny. She risks blacklisting herself from any type of romantic relationship at that point. Sure, guys want to be bros with the funny chick — maybe they wouldn't even mind putting one in her — but no one wants to date the funny chick. "Oh, Harper, you fucking kill me!

You just crack me up like the Liberty Bell. Buuutt... I'm not into you. You're weird enough to be sorta funny, but you're just too weird to date." The whole thing is a double standard, I tell you. Forget about the gender wage gap. The real issue is the social and biologically conditioning that causes everyone to think chicks can't be funny. Okay, I'm being a liiiiiittle bit dramatic here, but you get my point. Girls typically cite "funny" as a desired quality in a man. If a dude is funny, that usually makes him sexy, even if he looks like someone slapped a mosquito off his face with a heated hammer.

Is humor seen as a masculine quality? Even the class clown type guys don't want to date funny girls. You know, the type of guys who amazingly find some way to make anything into a sexual euphemism, or who always found ways of sticking miscellaneous objects to the ceiling of your history classroom. Is the idea of dating someone funnier than oneself intimidating? Pretty girls without a single original thought in their primped little heads are what's in demand. The type of girls who question nothing and who only elicit the emotion of lust. A guy might try putting up with a funny chick, but if she asks questions other than when the next episode of *The Big Bang Theory* will be on or has interests outside of naked celebrity selfies, no thanks: next suitor, please.

Oh, please. You've had boyfriends. You and Will were together for, what, a year?

Will and I were together for about a year, yes. Then he swallowed a bottle of anti-psychotics. Our relationship must have been *very* fulfilling. It was so overwhelmingly, fabulously wonderful that Will had reached the peak of his existence at the age of twenty-four. His parents assured me that the **situation** (what a cold, impersonal term that is) was beyond anyone's control, even Will's. Years of manic depression had finally robbed him of his will (fuck, poor word choice) to continue on. The multitude of medication changes, sleepless nights, and crippling student-loan debt only heightened his **situation**. According to his family and his doctors, there was nothing I could've done to help him.

Their lack of eye contact said differently.

The eyes at the funeral had said otherwise, too. It'd been impossible not to notice the furtive glances, the whispers. The accusations. Any time that I'd turned my focus away from the teary-eyed speaker at the podium (Will didn't want a priest or anything like that... he'd left specific requests — so, I guess the idea had been stewing for a while), I caught at least two pairs of eyes scrutinizing me. Have people no shame? It was the social equivalent of launching heavy, goober-covered spitballs at the back of my head. It's like as a species we no longer grow out of the child's mindset that staring at people isn't a big deal. Some of them probably wanted me to notice, though. Their eyes said, "I know what you did, and I do *not* approve! Why didn't you save him?"

Why. Didn't. You. Save Him.

If there were any circumstance that demanded I

leave my clown shoes at home, it'd be a funeral. Right? A funeral requires more sophisticated footwear, like Oxford's or high-heels. It's a time to be serious, sensitive, and reflective. Being the girlfriend (ex-girlfriend?) of the deceased implies that you say a word or two, no matter the brevity. Even the reading of a horribly written poem is welcomed and accepted. More poetry, *please*! I had no poetry to read when I approached that podium.

You would've thought it was open-mic night at The DC Improv.

Actually, it felt more like a roast. My brain has defensively suppressed the majority of garbage spewed from my mouth that day, but I hope to Zeus that I'm not the only human-being to make dick jokes or to use the term "butt-hurt" at a funeral service. On second thought, maybe I hope that I *am* the only person stupid enough to use such lowbrow terminology at a funeral. The multitude of collective gasps occurring that afternoon was almost musical: a symphony of censure.

You know, I can't blame anyone for assuming that my buffoonery is what flatlined Will's emotional battery. For all of the years I'd known him, he'd been a bit of a clown himself. In high school people would periodically ask us why we weren't dating. After years of rejection and loneliness, I guess we sort of both came to the conclusion of, "Might as well." Even in high school I knew about Will's **situation**. Instead of becoming all Dr. Phil about it, I cracked jokes. And I do *not* discriminate. Anyone and anything is fair game once I open my big stupid mouth. Will would joke back, so I never took the time to sit back and think about the possibility that he needed something more than an Eddie Murphy with titties. Well, that's not fair. Even Eddie Murphy has played **serious** roles successfully.

*You need to take life more **seriously**. You can't even self-reflect without being sardonic.*

This is why I needed to leave.

The decision wasn't that difficult to make, really. After I did all of my crazy-paranoid research to find the safest, most peaceful cities on the East Coast, I discovered South Harbor: a quiet coastal town in Maine. No one ever talks about Maine, so it must be pretty quiet. With a destination in mind, I then proceeded to cut all of my ties to home. This meant deactivating all of my accounts online and changing my cell phone number. No Twitter. No Instagram. So long, Facebook. I'd written a short but informative note for my parents explaining to them that I was safe, but just needed to be on my own for a while. There's a part of me that regrets not saying goodbye to the people that I love, but I know they would have tried to convince me to stay out of pity. Nope. I needed to get out before the constant reminders sucked away what was left of my sanity.

If nothing else, these city-folk will know nothing of my past. They won't know that I'm capable of joking someone to death (*for fuck's sake...*).

You do understand that you are now completely and utterly alone, right? Ruth is no longer just up the road from you. The fire department building isn't behind your house and open until three in the morning. Your parents aren't sleeping up the hall from you like they have been for the last twenty-four years (oh God, the crippling student loans!). This is the first time you have been completely on your own.

You. Are. Alone.

My eyes focus on the DVD filled box in front of me, and I suddenly remember where I am. I'm in a new place. I have a new apartment. I will soon (hopefully) have a new job. I have a new life.

Now, it's time to become a new and better person.

Slowly, I reach inside the box. Once *Being John Malkovich* is placed upon the counter, I know there's no going back.

CHAPTER 2
COGS AND PEGS

It's funny, really, the things that most people take for granted.

There's the obvious things like money, food, shelter, and family, but for a select few it goes much deeper than that. For some, simply being accepted among your peers is the equivalent of winning the million-dollar jackpot or accidentally catching a pop fly from your favorite hitter at a packed game. Unfortunately, for those miserable few who are excluded from enjoying life, every day is a virtual pop quiz based on faltering character and lack of self-confidence. To fail this test often means death.

Death is not a punishment, in this case, but a solution.

When one is denied the basic human rights that come with being an individual, a solitary peg in the numberless cog system that occupies the grand pin-wheel of existence, then what is the point of living? If every day is nothing but brooding inner turmoil and mind-numbing loneliness, then why go on? Life is supposed to be a burden that we all share and prop up collectively. Without the multiple legs needed to do so, then you will inevitably fall into nothingness, alone and forgotten. I know mental illness and other tragic factors are usually the culprit of these types of circumstances, but I say that the worst hand you could be dealt in the game of life is genetic defect.

Born broken.

I know that deformities and other handicaps don't necessarily make up a person morally or spirit-ually, but you could argue that it would most certain-ly shape him/her intellectually and logically. Not the deformities themselves, who protrude, puss, and pul-sate unapologetically without merit, but the people who don't have to endure them. So, basically 99.99999% of the existential human race.

Normal people are normal people simply because there are more of them.

It's really as simple as that. If every single person on the planet suddenly became indistinguishably dif-ferent, all the way down to the molecular level, then the very definition of "freak" would have little to no meaning. The fact that so many people are almost exactly the same is why people like me have to live day-to-day putting on a face, pretending to be what I'm not.

Normal.

The very idea of going out to a bar or coffee shop, walking up to a pretty girl, asking her if she wants a drink, and making light conversation is laughable. Sure, I could pursue romance on a strictly platonic basis, but I always let my insecurities block me from ever making any real connections with other people. It's not like I am too chickenshit to talk to women or anything childish like that. I could go out right now to The Ultra, a club on Cannon Drive where the bottle service and dancers are all dressed in sexy, neon-tinted lingerie, and find at least one girl who would find me attractive enough to share a cab home with. I'm not exactly being humble here, but with steely blue eyes, an athletic build, and curly blonde hair to boot, I wouldn't be the worst guy you could end up being a Tinder match with. Ironically, I could pick up just about any woman I wanted, given that I had the money for drinks. Yet, I would only be setting myself up for disaster.

I could pay a prostitute double and still get rejected.

I assume most people think I am gay, and I kinda get why they would think that. When you're fit, attractive, and not surrounded by women or chasing them, it's commonly assumed that you are either light in the loafers or are a total weirdo. Well, at least I can say that I'm not gay. While I make an impressive $1.15 above minimum wage and live paycheck to paycheck like most people, I wouldn't call myself broke, either. I get by with what I need and try not to let my mental anguish dictate my fiscal spending. How easy would it be to go out and buy a new motorcycle or car, only to feel happy for a day or two? Sure, I've thought about filling that empty void with material goods and other shiny things that would bring me momentary happiness, but in the end, those things are nothing but distractions. Not that I could do any of that without raking up some serious debt, but lucky for me, I take joy in the simpler things in life. Plus, there are things that even money can't obtain. Things that are paid for in emotional and physiological currency only.

Love does not accept credit.

Being only twenty-eight, I have yet to truly find out what it means to know true love. It is weird how you grow up as a kid encased in a glass bubble of narcissism and ignorance, and slowly, through experience, become a bigger and hopefully better person than before. Each mistake, good or bad, chips away at that glass bubble until eventually you are hatched into the real world like a newborn chick, where you acknowledge and accept a reality that exists wholly outside of yourself. It is impossible to crack that shell without knowing the sweet and sour taste of true love. They say that once the taste has reached your palate, a phantom hole is punched in the soft pink tissue of your brain, assuring that you never forget its sugary, yet tart, juices of passion and unchained desire. As much as one could argue that the love a family shares is just as good or as important as sexual love, I personally think that is thinking selfishly and not fully comprehending the psychological impact of growing old with shell all over your face.

I am almost thirty, and yet, I cannot technically call myself a man.

The experience that prematurely shattered my metaphysical shell, for better or worse, happened on a hot August afternoon when I was only eleven years old. The sky was spotted with the occasional wisp of a thin cloud or two but was generally clear and illuminated with blazing sunshine. The distant sound of lawn mowers and wind chimes filled my room as my eyes wearily slid open to gaze the mid-morning sunlight that showered me in white warmth. With a slight breeze blowing in to take the edge off, I woke up that morning immediately knowing that this was a picture-perfect summer day.

Being an only child, I was accustomed to playing with the other kids who lived in my tight-knit neighborhood of townhouses and decorative mailboxes while my mom was at work. There was Travis up the street; he had a go-cart and a bitchin' tree house. The Michaud twins two blocks over had a plethora of video games and movies at their disposal, but you had to put up with their constant bickering about who gets to do what. There was also Anthony, whose parents had a huge above ground swimming pool that all the other neighborhood kids would flock to when the temperature got anywhere above seventy-five degrees.

Standing in my muggy, clothing-littered room, I took all of three seconds to make up my mind of how to beat the unrelenting heat waiting for me outside. I kicked through piles of dirty laundry to look for my only pair of swimming trunks, hoping to Christ that they weren't stale and as hard as a board from last week's swim. Once I found them and gave them a quick sniff test, I quickly stuffed myself in, ate a strawberry Poptart that I had left on my book stand from the previous night, brushed my teeth, and headed out the door on my quarter mile walk to Anthony's. In my hurry to leave, I forgot to put on shoes, but quickly decided against going back for them. Bringing them along would only get them wet later.

With the sun lapping at my shoulders and back and the wind pushing the curly strands of messy morning hair off my sweaty face, I strolled through the quiet suburban streets with a feeling of total freedom and purpose. I stayed to the soft grassy shoulder of the road to keep the pink soles of my feet from sizzling on the freshly paved asphalt. It felt like the day was literally made for me, as if I had willed it in my sleep to be the perfect setting for goofing around all day in my buddy's pool.

That ten-minute walk in the sun was the last time I can remember being truly happy.

When I finally reached Anthony's house, I headed for the front door to see if he was home. After a few unanswered knocks, I heard the familiar sounds of splashing and yelling from the backyard. I jumped off the steps and went around the garage to let myself in through the back gate. There, enjoying the best of their youth, was Anthony, his older sister Brianna, and her friend Christie whom I was acquainted with through summer school after almost failing the fifth grade. She was a squeaky little blonde girl with a flat chest and a shrill voice. All summer I had to hear her squawk and complain about how she shouldn't even be in summer school because of her ADHD. As if having the attention span of a goldfish was an excuse to not to study.

Brianna, on the other hand, was the polar opposite of Christie.

Brianna was very smart and incredibly beautiful. Even at fifteen she was well figured and wore make-up only to accentuate her already stunning face instead of just trying to look older like most eager teenaged girls do. With shoulder length chestnut colored hair and long smooth legs, she would undoubtedly break many hearts as she drifted effortlessly through life as most flawlessly stunning women probably do. I had a major crush on her ever since Anthony and I met in third grade and first hung out at his place. In fact, when sleepovers were arranged, I always insisted that we stay at his house. I didn't come right out and tell him that I was obsessed with his sister and was only going to his house for the night to spy on her, but instead I pretended like my place was too lame for a sleepover. With my mom working as a registered nurse and my dad leaving us high and dry just after I was born, you could understand why we didn't have common luxuries like cable and Internet access.

I never felt like I was missing out, though. I always had plenty of friends and activities to keep me busy in my spare time. When all the other kids were busy with their own families, I would sometimes call my Mom at work and pester her to come home on her lunch break to give me a ride back to the hospital with her so I could hang out and play doctor when no one was looking. The one advantage to being an only child with a single mom who worked all the time is that you almost always got your way through means of sympathy. Most people can't say no to the idiot's bastard son.

Both girls were lounging in plastic lawn chairs in identical zebra-striped two-piece bathing suits, probably trying to tan, while Anthony was jumping around in the pool like he was on fire. Clearly irritated, both girls screeched and cursed as rogue waves of cold water from Anthony's spastic synchronized swimming routine doused them out of their flimsy plastic chairs.

"Hey, Antonio!" I yelled over as I made my way across the freshly cut lawn. "Keep horsin' around like that and there won't be any water left in that pool by sundown, R-tard."

"Oh, suck off, Nick! It's my damn pool, so I does as I please," Anthony joked back as he did an exaggerated doggy paddle towards the edge to meet me, once again causing a random shower of mist and rainbows to trail him across the water. "Best be nice to me if you want to be partaking in the fine poolery I have here." He slapped at the water like a happy seal as if to prove that it was in fact his pool and didn't belong to his parents — the property owners.

"Hey, Nick!" Brianna called over after running to get a towel from the patio, drying off her hair and face as she and Christie moved their chairs to avoid being further soaked. "Don't mind him, he's being a real goober today. You drop a kid on his head once and this is what you get."

"At least I wasn't adopted, turd burglar," Anthony retorted before I even had time answer back. Feeling he had won the debate, Anthony immediately proceeded to do shaky handstands in the water while his lower half swung around the air above the waterline like a severed pair of legs trying to Charleston.

After a good laugh at Antonio's expense, I climbed into the pool and finally began to enjoy the sticky, humid heat in the only way God had intended: surrounded by tepid, chlorine enriched water.

After an hour of slow-motion underwater fighting and fake drowning rescues, I started to get hungry. I told Antonio and the others that I had to run home and grab something to eat. I thanked them for letting me use their pool, and made my way up the ladder to leave.

Then, it happened.

As soon as I got to the top of the ladder, I felt significantly lighter. The warm breeze enveloped me, and for a second I hadn't even noticed that Anthony had pantsed me as I was climbing out of the pool. Blood rushed to my temples as I crouched and tried desperately to shrink into myself while still balancing on the steel ladder above the pool. A shriek and loud, sudden gasping were what snapped me out of my trance, but by then it was too late. The girls scrambled out of their chairs and ran into the house, the whole time screaming and chanting, "OH MY GOD!" while Anthony just stood in the pool slack jawed and silent.

I quickly skimmed my shorts out of the water without a word and put them on as I rushed towards the gate to leave.

As I crashed through the gate and ran for the open road, I heard Anthony yell to me — probably still standing in the pool. It was the last thing he ever said to me.

"DUDE, WHAT'S WRONG WITH YOUR DICK?!"

I ran home, bare feet pounding and scraping against hot pavement, all the while wondering what exactly he meant by that. My initial embarrassment was to the fact that my all-time crush and her loud-mouthed friend saw my shriveled family jewels after I had been splashing around in the icy waters of the pool. I don't think I need to explain what happens down there, but there was more to it than shrinkage. What should have been a barrage of teasing and laughter was instead a mad panic of confusion and disgust.

With the sounds of my tender skin slapping on the loose rock moving under my feet, my eardrums filled with the skull-thumping beat of my ever-quickening heartrate pounding ripples through my body. In a blind daze, I ran until silver specks filled my eyes and I could barely breathe. When I got home, I ran up to my room and locked the door. Later that day when my Mom got off from work, she noticed the trail of bloody footprints leading upstairs, and soon I was reliving the whole gruesome story.

She calmly sat and listened, but when I got to the part about being pantsed, her face dropped, and her posture grew rigid. I kept asking her feverishly, "Why, Mom? Why did they treat me like a monster?" and for several minutes she sat motionless across from me, staring down at the floor with black tears staining her once soft, rosy cheeks. Eventually, she grabbed a pen and paper off of the bedside mantel and wrote down one word. She slowly handed me the sheet. Through harsh, semi-toneless words, she told me to go to the library before they closed to look it up on their computers if I really wanted to know why. She apologized sobbingly for not being able to tell me more. I took the piece of lined paper and stared at the word printed on it in my mother's tear stained text.

Diphallia.

The word meant nothing to me upon initial viewing, but I had to know its meaning fast. So, I got dressed and ran the four blocks to the library with only twenty minutes until they closed. Quickly, I got on AskJeeves.com and typed in the word.

You know the old saying "ignorance is bliss?" Well, had I known that were true, I would have never looked up that word. Not that it would have fixed my problem; eventually I would have found out that most guys don't have to use both hands when they piss. It just would have been nice to enjoy that glorious innocent bliss for only just a little while longer. The parental block on the library's Internet wouldn't let me look at pictures, but I was able to get a definition from a medical website that summed up everything that I needed to know:

Diphallia: A rare congenital condition that causes a male to be born with two sex organs. It statistically occurs once in every 5.5 million births and is widely claimed that no two cases are identical.

In all the eleven years of my existence, I had only ever seen one penis.

Well...make that two.
My own.

I had never seen porn before and was strictly prohibited in what I could watch for movies by my Mom. The raunchiest movie I had seen up until that point was *Batman and Robin,* and besides the occasional costumed nipple and awkward chemistry between characters, there was nothing even remotely sexual throughout that entire train wreck of a film. I feel incredibly dumb saying this, but I had no idea that every other person around me had only one penis. I grew up in an area where sex-ed wasn't taught in public schools and teen pregnancy was the norm. I literally had nothing to reference but myself.

My immediate reaction to this disillusion was anger towards my mother for not telling me the truth sooner. She had to have known that I would find out that I was a freak once I learned basic anatomy. How dare she keep this a secret and leave me to find out about my physical retardation in the most inconvenient way possible? In my later years, I realized that she avoided telling me that I was different to keep me from feeling ashamed and also to keep me from assuming that my condition was the reason why Dad left so suddenly after I was born.

Well, lot of good that did. By the time the new

school year started, I would be even more of a social outcast than David Gerry: the smelly kid in home-room who thought he was a dinosaur and pretended to breathe toxic gas on people when they made eye contact. With only a little over a month left until school started up again, I had no idea how I was going to make it through the year, let alone the rest of my life, knowing that I was nothing but a side-show attraction.

On my long walk home, I prayed to God that the kids at school didn't find out about my extra member or would at least be open-minded and understanding about it.

Apparently, God was too busy to listen.
The next six years of school were pure hell.

From the very first day back from vacation, I was greeted by eager kids with shit-eating grins saying, "Hey! It's Double Dick Nick!" and "Here comes Nick, the amazing two headed boy!" I quickly learned that nearly everyone in my seventh-grade class had heard all about what happened at Anthony's pool over the summer. When people weren't laughing and calling me Nicky Pitchfork, I was constantly being asked stupid questions from other kids like, "When you pee, does it come out of both ends?" and "Can you tie them together like a bow?"

At first I ignored the taunting and tried to play it off like it wasn't a big deal, but when I got into high school two years later, the teasing became unbearable. I would drag myself out of bed every morning and ride the bus for forty minutes alone in a big empty seat by the front with the middle schoolers and alternative ed. kids. I arrived at school only to find crudely drawn portraits of me with elephant tusks between my legs all over my locker, Chinese finger traps stuffed through its vents, and random notes informing me that there was a spot reserved in hell for double dogging freaks like me. Not everyone was this cruel and impersonal, though. I had a few friends who never even so much as brought up my situation, but I always secretly felt they were only friendly with me out of pity.

Those long, desolate days throughout high school were incredibly lonely, but even more so, incredibly confusing.

While the rumor of my double indemnity was rampant throughout the school and probably the entire town, no one could deny that I was gradually blossoming into a real stud muffin. Since the day of my awkward unveiling, I had grown to a whopping 6'2" and had acquired quite the physique from years of extra-curricular activities like basketball, JROTC training, and various classes at the Y. Aside from being tall and muscular, I had thick, curly blonde hair that most girls pestered me to fondle in between classes. If my looks and hair were enough to get me a real girlfriend, I would never be alone, but we all know that no one ever finds true love by having strong shoulders and chiseled abs.

My good looks got me plenty of girlfriends, but none of them ever really loved me even if they had said they did. The ones who didn't know about my double angle dangle soon found out once they gossiped to their friends about who they were currently dating, and the ones who did know were a little too into catching a glimpse of the torn snake. I had one girl who bet me a coke while we were at the drive-in that she could fit them both in her mouth at the same time. I don't know if she was joking or just trying, rather clumsily, to be sexy. I barely entertained the idea before sheepishly changing the subject back to the film.

All in all, the most important thing I learned in school was to keep my head down and act like the constant ridicule and name-calling didn't bother me in the slightest. I could have found the kids who wrote those notes or drew those curly French mustache cocks on my locker and easily kicked their teeth in, but I knew that by doing so I would only be backing up the idea that I was indeed a freak. I knew the only way to make it out of high school alive was to stay quiet and take the jabs and corny insults from all the ignorant yokels with a smile on my face. To let anyone see me truly suffer would be an admittance of shame for being defective.

I wouldn't dream of giving anyone the satisfaction.

Once graduation rolled around, I eagerly made plans to move somewhere far, far away from everyone and everything I had ever known. College was never really an option for me, with my subpar grades and zero school scholarship offers, which was all fine. I never saw the point of going to college to accumulate insane amounts of debt when you're not even sure of why you are even going in the first place. Plus, I don't think I could handle sharing a dorm room with someone who would get accepted to the same "prestige" university as I would. The only natural solution I could foresee was packing up my stuff into my beat-up Chevy Lumina; heading five hours southeast to South Harbor, a booming seaside metropolis located near the southern border of the state, and to find a meager job to go with my predictably meager apartment.

I didn't care in the slightest about missing out on the college experience because all I ever wanted for years was to just be somewhere where no one knew about my hidden shame. How perfect would it be to be able to walk down a crowded street knowing that nobody had any idea that I had a split pipe in my pants? Having to work a pointless day job while living in a shitty one-bedroom apartment was a small price to pay for total comfort and social ambiguity. I could leave the past behind me and finally start a new life in a place where I was just another blank slate among templates of constant change.

Within a week of moving out of my Mom's and signing the lease to my new place on Plymouth Avenue, I managed to land a full-time job at Mona's Cleaners, a small family owned office cleaning company. Over the years, I worked my way up to shift manager. I never did make any new friends, but I did learn the beautiful layout of the rocky beaches just a mere two-mile walk from my apartment. I spend much of my off time from work walking the ocean line around the city, thinking about how much easier things are now that I have sanctuary in this coastal concrete grid. Yet, after nearly ten years of dusting and scrubbing dirty copiers and booger stained bathroom walls, I still tempt myself with the one burning question that frames my innermost thoughts always.

Will I ever find true love?

Then, just as I was nearly convinced that the answer was a heavy but anti-climactic NO, she came into my life.

Her name is Harper.

Chapter 3

Coffee Runs

Well, it's been a week. My supply of Ramen noodles is down to one lonely package of beef flavored "soup" that has nested itself at the bottom of my cupboard. All week I've been studiously hunched over the classified ads, but to no avail. Not having money slows down the job-hunting process. Like, "ate-too-much-cheese" slowness. Oh, the irony... Seems counterproductive, if you ask me. Since I can't afford to pay for internet service at the apartment and my neighbors have discovered that I've been "borrowing" their Wi-Fi (labeled "SxyRvrSde-Btchs"), I've just about used up all of my data.

I know it's idiotic to have a smartphone while you're living off Ramen noodles and loneliness, but without a phone, I wouldn't be able to answer any calls for potential job interviews. So, a lose-lose sitch-iation. The most promising job opportunity has been at a German themed pub called "Mein Schnucki," but in order to work there, I would have to be okay with exposing "mein titten" to the general public. Not only do I not want to tarnish my hiring potential for future jobs, but my rack, Biggie Smalls, is noticeably skewed to the right. And so, the search continues.

Go for another walk? Look for some more "now hiring" signs? I mean, you aren't accomplishing much by sitting around internally complaining like a whiny bitch. Go out and look.

What a wonderful idea: burn more calories than I'm capable of consuming. I'm no mathematician, but that's how a person loses weight. I've always been a bottom-heavy gal, and this is the first time since puberty that I've had to wear a belt to avoid looking like some thugalicious hoodlum or like I lost my ass in 'Nam.

With my data about used up and no money for a newspaper (do people even sell newspapers any-more?), venturing out into the business district is really my only option at this stage of the game. Calories be damned. Maybe I'll get lucky and there'll be some vendors at Buster's Big Stop handing out free samples of mystery meat. The peeling walls of this closet I live in are beginning the close in on me, an-yway. It's about time to meander out into the world.

Grudgingly, I push myself off of my pile of mis-matched blankets. Jesus-tap-dancing-Christ, I miss having a mattress. My back responds with a dull popping in agreement, and a low growling in my stomach reminds us all of why a mattress is out of the question at this point in our lives.

You gotta get a job first. Then when you get dee job, you get dee money. Then when you get dee money, you get dee mattress.

Don't quote that shit at me. I know I'm broke, but I won't have that kind of trash in my home. Maybe I should build my own drug regime? It seemed to work for Tony Montana...

I slip on a pair of flip-flops, snuggling the worn thongs between my toes and then decide that sneakers would be better. There's no way of knowing how long I'd be walking around the city, and with my shitty sense of direction, I'll probably become lost at least five times. Or ten. The last thing I need right now is a huge, pulsing blister between my toes. Sneakers it is.

After I lace up my red, tattered Chuck Taylors — the most iconic sneakers in existence — I can't help but notice how empty my apartment feels. How does a studio apartment the size of a low-income public-school classroom supply closet manage to feel barren? Granted, I could only bring what could be squeezed into Vlad the Impala, but all the essentials of life have come along with me. The living room/kitchen/bedroom space has been dominated by the old Panasonic television my grandmother gave me when I was thirteen and the peristyle of DVDs and CDs surrounding it. Most places have at least a few pictures or posters on the walls. The most decorative thing on my walls is the patch above my "bed" where the paint has peeled in the shape of a sagging scrotum (in my head, since I am utterly and completely **alone**, I now think of bedtime as "tea time"). The only window in the apartment provides a most glorious view of the dumpster out back and of the classy ladies the dude upstairs brings home while they are on their smoke/alcohol breaks from the questionable activities occurring above me. Those dames always provide some insightful background banter ("Herpes isn't a big deal; you just get a rash sometimes."), and yet...

Taking one last look at the desolate dungeon that is my apartment, I step out into the late summer air to seek better days.

Dream, Scarface. Dream.

***

The sun has almost finished today's journey and the shadows are growing taller. My own journey, however, is nowhere near finished. In the last five hours, I've gone into at *least* fifty establishments, filled out *thirty* applications, and have asked to speak to *ten managers*. The responses ranged from: "We aren't looking right now," to "Fill out an application," and my *absolute* favorite, "We'll call you." The best part is that most of the places were restaurants. The emptiness of my gut was only exemplified by the sounds of utensils against plates and the smells of grease and gluttony. How cruel is that?

For once in my life, I find myself longing to be behind the wheel of Vlad. I'd gladly forget about all the times he has overheated on me, and I would absolutely *relish* the feeling of the rogue spring prodding my perineum. However, gas means money, and Vlad is uninsured as of two days ago. Walking will soon become a big part of my life, I think.

The sidewalk ahead of me seems to grow with each passing second, stretching ahead of me like some tripped out cartoon. The sea air is so heavy I can taste it, which only causes my empty gut to bitch and moan some more. Salt is an element of food, after all. Since the sidewalk and the majority of shop fronts are made of dull red brick, there really aren't any true distinguishing features to my surroundings. Am I even moving at this point?

Walking through the city at night is probably my least favorite activity. It even outranks getting a pap smear. Give me a week's worth of paps before making me walk alone at night, *please*! I'd run to the office with open legs. I mean, I guess it could be nice (walking in the city at night — not a week's worth of pap smears... unless you're into that sort of thing); there are far fewer people cluttering up the walkways — God knows people drive me crazy — but it's also when the less-human inhabitants come out of hiding. The weirdos trying to sell, or score, the currently trending drug. College kids with too much money and nowhere near enough responsibility and/or ambition. I think I'd prefer hookers over college bros and hos. At least hookers typically know their true worth.

As I ponder the possible strategies for determining the market price of a standard-grade hooker, I realize that I can't remember which direction leads to my apartment. Fan-fucking-tastic. Why do all of the streets in a city look identical!? You'd think the city planner would've included some type of variety to the landscape to make navigation easier. Nope. I remember passing an old granola-looking dude with bird crap streaked through his matted hair singing about organic crops and corporate bailouts, there was a Starbucks at some point, and the university isn't far from my apartment...

An even more terrifying realization backhands me: I'm the only person on the sidewalk. How the hell did that even happen!? How is it even possible for a living, breathing humanoid to not notice that there are, I don't know, **zero** people around it? My heart cannonballs into my stomach. I guess my mental panic attack about the oncoming Night distracted me more than I'd thought.

The sun is no longer visible in the sky, having drawn the curtain of Night behind it. At what point did everyone around me leave?!? Am I *that* unobservant!? Has my slight starvation begun to eat away at my brain already!? The job-hunting will have to end for tonight; I have to get home as fast as possible. Nighttime means darkness, and darkness means mystery. Mysteries end with young women with broken vaginas, bludgeoning, bodies in ditches... During the hours of Night, I find it more and more difficult to know for sure what my overactive imagination is conjuring up on its own and what is actually "real." You know how when you're a kid and you watch scary movies for the first time, they seem so realistic? All of those horrible Plaster of Paris creations and lazily done animatronics have a life of their own. To you, the child, that is real life.

Most people grow out of this phase of their lives. Or so I've heard. More connections are made in the brain, and the part that controls decision-making, problem solving, and rationality finally develops as we reach adulthood. My brain has not yet reached this point of development. Honestly, I'm not sure that it ever will. Those cardboard monsters and too red to be real blood packets? Those are all still very real to me. Being afraid of the dark in your twenties is sort of funny, but in a "piss your pants now, laugh later," sort of way.

I keep my eyes ahead and do my best to not think about the growing shadows surrounding me. In my head, I play my current favorite Frank Zappa album (for the hundredth time this week, I've lost my headphones) and try to ignore the subharmonic sounds of the night: the whine of electricity from the closed shop signs, the whispers of the unknown, and my own shallow breathing.

The shop passing on my left is an "oddity shop." It's one of those places where you could find racist cartoons from the 20's or a petrified horse penis. *Why* did I take this route!? The shop is the type of building that is unsettling even during the brightest of summer days. The faded Old English lettering is a dirty gray color, but a few patches of dark brown are splattered throughout. I'm not sure if the paint was originally a dark brown, if the shop owners created this faded look purposely, or if the brown coloring is some other substance I'd rather not know about.

Looking at the shop causes me to imagine a musty "old" smell. Like the smell of an untouched attic, or the home of an elderly old man who has decided on his own terms, or by obligation, that housekeeping is no longer a priority. I've never gone into the shop, but it looks like it would be very dry and cool. And full of Lovecraftian monsters. Of course.

*Why are you analyzing a creepy old building???
Keep your eyes ahead and your feet moving.*

My body tenses up as a piece of trash gallops down the sidewalk behind me. It's hard to believe that this street is usually bustling with activity. College students, the locals (who hate the college students, despite the fact that they bring in the majority of the city's revenue), crazy protesters who seem to protest the opposing group of protesters more than an actual cause (I can't even remember what their cause originally was — I wonder if *they* can even remember), and an occasional musician playing an out-of-tune guitar and singing in an even more out-of-tune voice.

So what, no jokes?

Being alone – at night – in a city — no matter *how* small — isn't comedy hour! Well, unless it's New York, I guess. Everything is *closed*! There are *no human-beings* around. I can't even remember how to get back to my apartment.

But, you know, a funeral is the perfect time to be funny. When a person close to you opens up about his struggles with depression, now THAT'S the perfect time to make a fart joke...

Before I have time to play any more mental gymnastics, the street light above me winks (queefs [see, I can make jokes that aren't about farts]) out of existence, and I take off like a cowardly bat out of

Hell. I barely feel the pavement beneath me as I sprint down the sidewalk. There's a shop light in the distance, and I instantly decide to get to that building as fast as is humanly possible. I don't give myself the chance to think about how the light could actually ly be helping some deranged psychopath see his tools while he skins newborn puppies. No time for that shit. No wonder my baseball coaches always put me in as a pinch runner; the distance between myself and the open shop, a coffee shop, closes in what feels like seconds. Truly impressive, considering how scared shitless I am.

Lucky for me, the door is a "push" rather than a "pull" because I heave myself at that sucker like a lineman. The jolly jingle of the bell doesn't cover the sound of the barista gasping at my dramatic entrance. Her dark eyes are wide as she gazes upon my panting, fear-drained self.

I straighten up and wipe the sweat from my forehead. "Hey, sorry to freak you out. I just... really need a macchiato right now." I try my best *I'm-not-a-psycho-I-promise* smile and gently approach the counter. The barista's expression softens, but I can tell that she still thinks I'm a little weird. Nothing new.

"So, a macchiato? What size? Any flavoring?" The barista, Megan — according to her nametag — tries her best retail smile as she approaches her register. I can tell that she's strategically keeping the distance between us wide enough so that she can make an emergency escape if necessary. Or to provide her with enough space to kick me in the ovaries.

I scan the menu, remembering my depleted bank account. "Well, on second thought, I think a tall iced coffee will have to do for tonight. Caramel, please. Light cream." As I swipe my debit card, I feel my sphincter clench at the thought of negative funds, but I feel like scaring the girl shitless is reason enough to buy something.

Damn my sense of decency.

She leaves the register momentarily to work her barista magic. When she comes back, she seems a little more relaxed, and her smile seems more authentic. There's still an undertone of fear on her face, but who could blame her?

I accept my coffee, doing my best not to have our fingers make physical contact and further freak her out. Raising my cool cup of jitter juice, I tell her, "Thank you; you are a gentleman and a scholar," before finding an empty seat to sulk in.

I sit down with my back facing the window, wondering if my drink will turn into a salted caramel iced coffee if I start to sob into it. A whole day spent hunting for a job and this is how it ends: lost and freaked the fuck out in a coffee shop drinking a coffee that I can't even afford. And, of course, there's Megan behind the service counter, who's probably texting her manager about the deranged bitch running into the shop in the dead of night demanding coffee. It probably wouldn't be appropriate to ask her for a job application at this point. There's *nothing* left tonight.

Or in my bank account.

As I hang my head in defeat and fight off the

tears threatening to add more zest to my drink, the bulletin board catches my attention. No, it isn't one of the fifty "professional" looking *Drummer Wanted* signs that catches my interest or even the *Booty Yoga Class* advertisement. There's a handwritten note tacked up among the business cards and event flyers. Being mindful to move slowly so I don't freak Megan out even more, I move closer. The clumsy handwriting reads:

> Now Hiring cleaning professionals.
> No experience necessary. Must be able to work evening hours. Mona's Cleaning. Call any time! Ask for Angelica.

My heart begins to beat a little faster. I don't even care that a company called "Mona's Cleaning" says to ask for a person who isn't named Mona. I pull my cell phone out of my pocket: 10:05pm.

Well, the note does *say to call any time, and it* is *for an evening job.*

Without a second thought, I dial the number written on the note, close my eyes, and wish for a miracle.

CHAPTER 4
LäTHER

I woke up today much like I did on that seemingly perfect summer morning back in the days of the hidden hydra. The sun was spilling into my dusty apartment through the makeshift American flag curtain hung cockeyed over the chipped and splintered window frame looming directly above my disheveled single size bed. I open my eyes to find tiny dust particles dancing and drifting on invisible waves of unseen energy streaming past my eyes, selectively illuminated by a tiny slot of light hanging just a couple of feet in front of my upturned face. The sounds of lawnmowers and wind chimes are replaced by the sounds of traffic and the miscellaneous murmuring of distant conversation from the busy sidewalk down below. Rubbing my sticky, sleep dusted eyes, I force myself to roll out of bed and groggily start my mundane morning routine.

After taking a shower, brushing my teeth, and

sorting through piles of wrinkled laundry until finding semi-clean clothes to wear, I sit down to a bowl
of Mini-Wheats at my tiny kitchen counter and
watch random YouTube videos on my phone until it
is time to drive to the address that I will be working
at for the day. Every weekday my boss Angelica texts
me the new address of where our crew will be meeting up to do a job. As shift manager, it is my responsibility to organize the meeting and transportation of
supplies. After informing the other four crew members of that night's meeting location, my routine is to
make a stop by the company's storage unit and pick
up the vacuums and other cleaning supplies. This
trip to the storage unit is delayed today by a call from
Angelica informing me that Ronaldo, a quiet, middle
aged Filipino man with a wispy black mustache and
the word *precious* tattooed on the left side of his
neck, was no longer hired on and that a new girl
would be taking his place today on my shift. I write
down the name and number on the back of a bank
receipt that was in my front pocket then head out for
the day after texting the new girl an address and time
to meet.

The best part of my late afternoon is the drive to
work. As of late, I have been blasting Frank Zappa's
masterful live album *Hammersmith Odeon* everywhere I go, always managing to turn the heads of the
passing after-work foot traffic clogging the sidewalks
when the song "Muffin Man" comes screeching and
tearing out of the crackly, ten-inch factory speakers
installed in the Lumina. With my curls springing and

twisting all around my head, I roll down all the windows and crank the stereo, letting my thoughts and usual anxieties drown in a gust of city air and awe-inspiring, electrified guitar solos played over impossibly orchestrated pieces of multi-layered music that will sadly never truly be replicated ever again. The thought always hits me deep when I think about things that are so ahead of their time that they are dismissed as trash because of close minded critics deciding for everyone what is "acceptable content."

To quote Zappa himself:
"Without deviation from the norm, progress is not possible."

I jam on over to the storage unit, pack up the supplies, then head to the address which turns out to be an insurance firm just two blocks from my favorite Chipotle spot. I pull into the parking lot and notice that almost all of my crew is here waiting outside the locked glass plated doors of the two-story office building. They are standing in a loose circle, some leaning against the doors smoking and others using their phones under the naked white glow of halogen floodlights mounted to the crest of the giant metal door frame. My headlights splash across their faces as I pull into a vacant spot and begin unloading the numerous Simple Green containers from the back seat of my car.

"Yo! Took ya long nuf, man. Need some help wid'ose?" asks Bobby as he throws down his still smoldering cigarette butt and walks over to meet me at the rear door. Bobby is a sickly skinny white kid in his early twenties who spends way too much time smoking pot and updating his Twitter feed with narcissistic photos of himself rolling oversized joints and counting "wads" of cash, fancy camera filters masking his pock marked cheeks and grimy, yellow teeth. The most intriguing thing about Bobby, though, is his self-proclaimed passion for singing and rapping when in reality he is completely tone deaf. Whenever he tries to show off his skills and drops an improvisational melody, trying to seem creative and spontaneous like Usher or R. Kelly, it always comes out sounding like a dyslexic, off-key nursery rhyme that even Bjork would laugh at. His eyes are always shiny and glazed like two tiny, pink crystal balls worming with veins, rolling around in the deep, sunken sockets of his peanut shaped skull. Never ashamed at the fact that he is clearly higher than a space probe, Bobby's obvious lunch break antics and odd conversation are only tolerable because he shows up for work on time every day and displays a moderately good work ethic. Aside from forcing me to hear him duet with Drake every night for six to nine hours straight, thanks to that portable stereo he always brings in, I actually enjoy his non-confrontational banter and choose to look the other way on some of his personal habits outside of work.

"Sorry. I got a call from Angelica about getting a new girl tonight," I say as I start passing vacuum hoses and window cleaner bottles back to him over my shoulder. "Is she here yet by any chance?"

"Nah, I ain't seen no one but Sofia n' Luciana. I knew Ronaldo got 'is dumb ass fired when I din' see him ride in wit Sofia like he usually does." Sofia and Luciana are two old Colombian ladies who only talk to each other in rapid, rolling tongue Spanish while on the job. Anytime they have to talk to anyone else who wasn't Colombian or Mexican, they would speak perfect English with only the slightest hint of their South American roots bleeding through the forced tongue of a foreign land.

Taking a handful of mops from out of the passenger seat, Bobby adds sourly, "Tha guy gets blackout drunk on da weeken n' goes roun' pickin fights at bars down on da borwalk. I bet ya twenty bucks that he be hittin on some dude's chick n' got 'is ass knocked out on da beach. Prolly down at South 'Arbor Genral righ now ina ajustable bed laid up ina coma."

"Angelica didn't say why," I say back to him as we cart the stuff across the big, empty parking lot over to the sliding glass doors. "All I know is that we are getting a new person, so if you see someone at the doors, make sure to let me know." I get the pass code out of my pocket and unlock the doors, propping them open for everyone to begin unloading the supplies as I search for the switch that turns on the main lights.

The main lobby of the building is lined with padded chairs and desks much like an upscale bank or a lawyer's firm. In the center is an information kiosk filled with brochures and paperwork crowned with a huge poster of the company logo being held by a very pretty woman with nice tits. All in all, it isn't a huge lobby by any means, but definitely has a lot of area to cover. With dozens of ten-foot plate glass windows divided between both floors and numerous offices snaking down and around the building, the first floor alone will make for quite a long night. Once everyone gets their collapsible carts stocked, we pick our areas and go to work.

After fifteen minutes in the front lobby disinfecting tabletops and counters with "Jumpman" playing for the third time in a row off in the adjacent office, I hear a soft knocking on the glass doors directly to my right. "Must be the new girl," I think as I turn around to make my way to the doors.

Then, I see her.

Wearing a plain black V-neck t-shirt and dark blue jeans with her long, blood red hair tied back in a loose ponytail, she stands just beyond the doors in a pale halo of light. My heart jumps in my chest as I am taken aback by how incredibly beautiful her sharp cheekbones and hourglass figure are even at a distance. As the distance between us lessens, I can see her eyebrows are sculpted so exquisitely, even Michelangelo would be impressed. Even through the splotchy, finger stained glass, her flawlessness is clearly visible. I glide across the lobby and, with ghostly fingers, unlock the door and hold it open.

"Hi," she starts as she walks past me into the lobby, her voice firm but friendly in tone. "Are you Nick?"

"Yes," I reply in a squeaky bark after taking far too long to respond. Standing just a few feet from her and trying my hardest not to stare, I clear my throat and snap myself back into manager mode. I quickly take out the bank receipt that I had scribbled her name down on earlier and say, "Well...Harper, nice to meet you." I extend a shaky wet palm to her and we shake hands. "You must be the newest member of the crew. Did Angelica give you the rundown of what we do?" I ask as I lead her over to my cart by the long row of counters.

"Yeah, I think so. She said something about organizing a kidnapping of one of the CEO's of this company. I brought the ropes and chloroform that she said we would need, but I couldn't find a hacksaw. Did you bring one by any chance?"

I freeze in my tracks and slowly turn around, wide eyed and confused. Her green eyes sparkle up at me with an innocent beauty that, for a second, stunts me. Two butterfly winged eyelashes delicately framing a pair glistening emerald stones. I try subtly to read her expressionless face until a smile slowly unfolds across her glossy lips, and she says, "Just kidding. Just a little joke to lighten things up. I didn't mean anything by it. Sorry." She quickly breaks eye contact and looks down at the floor as if embarrassed. I watch her hand drift reflexively to the back of her head. She notices me watching her and pulls her hand back down to her hips.

Sensing her awkwardness, I push out a chuckle and say, "Ooh, I see. I wasn't expecting that. No offense taken. Had I known we would be committing a felony, I would have brought two hacksaws. My mistake." She breaks her stare from the floor to flash me a faint smile. Her mahogany painted fingers play with a loose medallion that hangs elegantly around her neck as I try hard to come up with the words to break this awkward tension, but I can find none.

After what feels like minutes, I finally say, "Well, since I don't have any extra carts, I guess you and I will have to buddy up for the night. I will make sure to bring in an extra one for you tomorrow."

"Sounds great," she says quietly, her cheeks rosy and lips slightly pouty. Her gaze then shifts to the tiny yellow cart full of brushes and chemicals. "Where do I start first?"

"I was just wiping down all the tables and stuff. After that, I will probably wash the windows. Here." I hand her a couple rags and bottle of off brand window cleaner. "If you want to get started on the windows, that would be great." She takes the rags and bottle and, without a word, strides across the desk littered lobby to start her first task. I watch her walk away, ponytail bobbing and hips gliding, while my mind flips through a Rolodex of countless scenarios where she would be mine. Voices and images bleed into my thoughts and for a second, I feel a warm tingle building up in my chest. I know that I am being completely superficial, having only met her five minutes prior, but it isn't unnatural to appreciate un-attainable things. Some of the voices tell me to talk to her, make her laugh, ask her out for lunch, and even comment on how she probably is new to the city and needs a friend. As always, the loudest voice, in the end, is the one saying, "She will find out you are a freak. Why bother?" That is the end of my day-dreaming.

Time for work.

***

An hour went by without any conversation, just the overly repetitive sounds of Future "singing" warbly, nonsensical ramblings of sweet nothings drifting in from the next room. Suddenly, Bobby comes walking in and sees Harper bent down scrubbing a corner of the window's painted metal framing.

"Gaht Damn," he harshly whispers at me once he gets over to where I'm standing by the copiers. "Dat da new chick?"

"Yup, her name is Harper," I say as I continue to scrub the huge coffee stain that I have been busying myself with for the last ten minutes.

"You gonna call dibs on dat, or does she gaht a boyfriend?" he asks, not taking the volume of his voice into consideration. With no subtlety whatsoev-er, he proceeds to turn and stare at her as if through sheer mind power he could metaphysically slide a finger down her crack from across the room. "Mos bitches dat hot are either taken, or ape shit crazay.

You would hafta' put a ring on an ass like dat," he says, waggling his eyebrows and flashing a crusty, nicotine stained smile at me.

"I have no idea, Bobby. Why don't you ask..."

Then from behind us, Harper cuts in from across the lobby with, "No, he didn't call dibs and as for my ass, it only gets a ring on it after a long poop." She stands facing us with her arms crossed in a gesture of waiting as we both freeze in place like dime store mannequins.

"Oh, well shit, I don' mean nuttin like..." Bobby starts, his crusty lips flapping, exposing filmy, grey gums and a hairy, purple tongue. He stammers on as she strides across the tiled room to join the conversation. I am expecting him to get a slap or kick in the sack, but instead she comes over and continues to speak.

"A suave, sophisticated man such as yourself must only deal with the highest caliber of ladies, am I wrong?" Her voice slowly turns into a cockney British accent as the sentence rolls on.

Bobby can tell she is being sarcastic, and immediately his demeanor changes. With almost a foot in height difference between them, Bobby leers over her as she stands unflinchingly in front of him, waiting for an answer.

"Yur' fuckin righ' I do," he answers, chest puffed up and chin raised in his best Big Man pose. He literally inflated himself to prove he was much stronger and better than her. "Why, jus las night I was wit a shorty dat I met at the Ultra Club, and we bumped uglies til' like 2 a.m., or whatever. I had er e'ry which way, beggin for dat D." He ends with an attempt to high five me, even laughing at his own pathetic anecdote, but I just stare at him in disbelief at the lack of manners he is completely unaware of having. I can tell that he has no idea how dumb he looks and is really just boasting for the new girl, who probably thinks that he is slightly retarded in a medical sense.

Just as I am about to tell him to shut up and get back to work, Harper smiles, abandoning her previous British accent, and slyly says, "Every which way, huh? So, you had her upside down in a pile driver? Maybe bent over the edge of the bed for intense doggy style penetration? Please, do go on."

Bobby is noticeably caught off guard by her reaction to his egocentric bragging, but being the low life dick wipe that he truly is, keeps talking.

"I dun know bout any pile drivers, but I was defley beating up dat puss like it owed me money. But I ain't fuckin wit doggy style. Not big on da smell, ya know?"

Harper's face twitches in surprise. The left side of her mouth pinches downward and one of her dark eyebrows becomes even more arched. "The smell? What are you talking about? Are you saying that those classy broads you pick up at the club don't wash their assholes?"

Bobby's face goes as blank as a bowl of day old oatmeal; clearly this is the first time that the thought has been forced across his mind. Finally, after looking around the room helplessly like the answer would be held up on a sign by that woman with nice tits, he says, "Nah... I just...Nick, back me up here, yo. Ya know what I'm sayin, righ bruh?"

They both turn and wait for my response. I had been so wrapped up in the ridiculousness of their conversation that I am not prepared for any sexual questioning. Usually when I am in this type of situation, I have loaded answers ready for a quick response. So, being the ultra-virgin that I am and not wanting to further the conversation, I say, "Alright guys, it's time to get back to work. Bobby, if you're done in that room, you can go upstairs and give Luciana and Sofia a hand. Harper and I will take care of the bathrooms on the first floor before meeting you guys up there."

"Yessir!" he says in an overly feminine lisp and limp handed salute, obviously making fun of my unwillingness to defend his macho man status, and then proceeds to pack up his cart while Harper and I walk to the first-floor bathrooms located just beyond the long, oak reception desk.

Inside the men's room, we both grab rags and toilet bowl cleaner and each pick from one of four stalls. After several minutes of just the sounds of labored scrubbing and the scraping of dried boogers reverberating off the dull, grey walls and porcelain, I clear my throat and try to make small talk.

"So," I start, pausing momentarily from peeling the long, bloody loogie I was working on, "are you from South Harbor, or did you move here from out of state?" I pause and wait for a reply, but when I feel her resistance to answer, I say, "I'm from upstate my-self…"

"Actually," she says, cutting me off with her de-layed response, "I'm from Iraq. I recently moved to America to recruit child soldiers for the terrorist sect that I'm in back home. How do you feel about Mu-hammad, Nick?"

I can't see her face, but I know she is joking with me again. Yet, I still stumble to answer. "Uh…I feel…good?" I finally say, feeling like an idiot for try-ing to be friendly with someone so far out of my league.

She giggles at this and says, "Good answer, Infi-del. Seriously, though, let's talk about anything ex-cept the past. Like, what kind of music are you into? Please don't tell me you listen to that audible garbage that DJ Booty Stank was spinning out there."

Surprised, I quickly try to think of how many girls my age weren't completely obsessed with Drake or Future, and then say, "Well, I don't listen to much newer music, mostly classic prog rock. You know, stuff like King Crimson, Rush, Frank Zappa…"

I hear the door directly adjacent to the stall I am in slam open and in an instant, Harper is standing over me with the bewildered, wide eyed expression of someone who just won an unlimited supply of Star-bucks coffee.

She curls her little fists around the scraper, twist-ing it compulsively, and screams, "WAIT, WHAT?! *YOU* like Zappa too?!"

***

For the next six hours, we talked about everything from music, film, and television to pet peeves and philosophy. Aside from agreeing that Zappa was, without a doubt, the greatest musician/composer of the 21st century, we also shared a fondness for Indian pop music. Even agreeing on what bands we hated, both of us admitted that Bob Dylan was a mediocre song writer with a pension for playing scrabble with his own lyrics. For movies, we discussed at length how Quentin Tarantino is the only mainstream director making real films anymore and talked about our love for the amazing production quality in older films like *Eraserhead* and John Carpenter's *The Thing*. And while we could agree on most movies, she adamantly denied that *Scarface* was anything but a poorly written snuff film condoning the actions of a complete asshole. We shared a love of stand-up and sketch comedy, listing off names and acting out scenes from some of our favorite bits and sketches. This led us to talk extensively on the moral decay and self-absorption of most people of our generation, often citing Jimmy Fallon's popularity as proof.

The thing we disagreed on, or at least didn't have in common, was our choice in reading material. She professed a love of the horror greats like Stephen King and Lovecraft while I admitted to reading mostly science fiction, citing Philip K. Dick as one of my favorites. We rattled off countless names of books for each other to check out and by the time Bobby came down to tell us that the second floor was done, we had enough reading material between the two of us to last a single person years.

I broke conversation long enough to throw him my keys and tell him that we were just finishing up, asking him to start loading up the supplies into my car if he had nothing else to do. Finally sensing the amount of time that slipped past us in our seemingly short conversation, we rushed through the rest of the bathroom so it looked at least somewhat acceptable. Joining the others outside in the cool summer night, I locked up the front doors and helped Bobby with loading up my car.

Once everyone hands me their paperwork, we say our goodbyes and, one by one, the crew starts walking towards their vehicles to leave. I am about to leave when I notice Harper walking off towards the roadway. I yell to her and ask if she wants a ride, but she stops only long enough to politely decline and ask me if I will text her the address of the next job later. She looks back at me through the dim, hollow aura of the overhead dome lights and says, "Goodnight, Infidel." She flashes me a smile that makes my heart halt painfully in my chest. Reluctantly, I get in my car and drive off in the opposite direction, her tiny, red-lighted frame slowly shrinking to nothing in my rearview mirror.

That smile told me everything that I needed to know.

I float home on a fuzzy, dotted roadway in a magic, translucent box that used to be my Lumina in complete awe of what just happened. In all my life, I have never met someone so compatible with me on almost every level. Our views on everything from the ego machine that is social media to the sad manipulative commercials disguised as heartwarming documentaries by conniving corporate sponsors all coincide perfectly. If I had shared these opinions with anyone else, I would surely run the risk of getting punched in the face or landing a pricey sexual harassment charge. For the first time since I found out how different I am, I feel like I am not alone. Years and years of conflicting opinions and shaming myself for what I can't help have left me cynical and without much hope in anything. Even now, knowing that I have met someone amazing who actually likes me, I can't truly enjoy it.

Unless she happens to have two vaginas, I have no chance of being with her.

Having had way too much fun talking so freely with her, I grudgingly accept that being friends is better than nothing.

***

When I get home, I eat a dry bologna sandwich and get ready for bed, the whole time distracted with the thoughts of things that would never be. I climb into bed and for a while I toss and turn, too excited to sleep with the promise of seeing her again tomorrow. Against my better judgment, I pick up my phone off the end table and send a quick text to her, hoping that she isn't in bed. The tiny screen illuminates the huge, toothy grin I have as I punch at imaginary letters, and I immediately regret hitting send once it is all over.

Oh well, I think to myself as I set down the phone, lay back into bed, and start to embrace sleep. The sounds of distant traffic and sirens fade into white noise as my last thought for the night spins around the endless corridors of my damaged psyche.

What do I have to lose?

Chapter 5
Texting and Driving

Nick's taillights blink out of view, and it's in this moment that I remember the twilight trek ahead of me. The blackened sky is moon-free tonight, meaning my only source of light is the chain of streetlights scattered along the empty sidewalk. What's it called when the moon can't be seen? A New Moon? Of course, the first night of my job would fall on this day of the moon cycle. The universe wouldn't have it any other way. My life: the laugh track free sitcom.

I pull the hood of my sweatshirt over my head, creating blinders against the hollowness, and go gently into the night.

Why did you turn down a ride home?? Not only would that have saved you wasted calories that you aren't consuming, but it would have saved you *from another walk home alone — **in the dark** — in this hipster-infested city!! What were you thinking?? Were last night's wild and crazy times not enough for you? You ready for round two? I hope you brought a spare pair of underwear.*

Yeah, another stroll into the blackness of the city isn't what I wanted to pencil in for the evening, but I'd known that this would be inevitable when I was hired on for an evening job. I mean, a business isn't going to change its hours because the new girl has an irrational fear of the dark, right? Vlad is still uninsured and we're without gas money, so my feet are my only form of transportation until further notice. Time to suck it up and hum sweet nothings to myself to override the darkness and the anxious drumming of blood in my ears.

*But, you were offered a ride! Not only were you offered a ride, but you were offered a ride by a person with a Y chromosome who isn't too shabby to look at and who happens to like **FRANK-FUCKING-ZAPPA**! How many people have you met in your limited lifetime who have even heard the name Frank Zappa? Even old people respond with the typical, "Oh, I've heard of him, but I never actually listened to him." This could be a one-in-a-million shot, Harper. One in a million. He is probably cranking that shit in his car right now. The fuck you thinking, Harper? The. Fuck.*

Okay, so I'll be fair. Nick isn't a bad looking guy. Alright, he is more than not bad looking; he's so attractive, I think that I've started to ovulate. He's almost a little *too* good looking, like he walked out of an Nsync poster (wasn't one of them named Nick, actually? Or was that the Backstreet Boys?) and decided to go incognito by not shaving for a week, throwing on a pair of worn loose-fitting jeans, and getting a job for a cleaning company in a quiet city. Nah, that's not quite right. That hyperbole makes him sound like he looks like some kind of pussy. Nick looks like the lovechild of Justin Timberlake and Sacha Baron Cohen (shit, is he Jewish?? I called him an infidel...). Handsome as hell, but in no sense "pretty." Guys who are prettier than me automatically lose points on the attractiveness scale due to my competitive spirit. Regardless, he looks like the type of guy all the hot cheerleaders with bitchin' tits would willingly throw themselves at.

The type of guy who would never love me.

Love?

Okay, the type of guy who would never ask me to the movies. The type of guy who wouldn't want to attack the pink fortress even if it were last call during his worst case of blue balls. No way, no how.

Tonight was your first night around new people. That is, if you don't count poor Megan at the coffee shop. What happened to toning down the "comedy?" Your first complete sentence to your new manager was sarcasm. You embarrassed Bobby-Ray Bitches as he flaunted and fluffed up his tail feathers for the other male in the room. Your job is to clean toilets. Those people have enough shit to deal with without having to listen to your antics.

Bobby needs some humiliation in his life. In no way, shape, or form do I regret putting that pasty cracker in his place. He is a disgrace to Caucasians everywhere. I never felt "white guilt" as an adult and found that term to be a little snobby and ill informed. Then, I met Bobby. Now, I'm so sorry for what the white community has done to black culture.

But... maybe I shouldn't have been so sarcastic around Nick. The guy was kind enough to attempt to make small talk with me while we cleaned a filthy fart factory.

Small talk? A conversation of six hours has graduated to a rank higher than small talk. Small talk is when you talk about the weather, who is going to win the World Series (even when it's not baseball season), or how much the president is fucking up. Literature — unless it is the newest racy romance novel — is usually not a topic discussed during "small talk."

It feels like it's been years since I've had a *real* conversation about subjects that matter. Not which celebrities are boning each other or mundane personal information ("You know, my daughter is in the first grade now...her teachers tell me she has the communication skills of a second grader..."). Never have I met another twenty-something year old without a social media account. Well, okay — so I *did* have accounts awhile back, but I deactivated everything within the first forty-eight hours of Will's death. There were far too many photos. Too many comments. Too many reminders.

This begs the question:
What is *Nick* hiding from?

What's Nick's reason for not using social media? Is it for the simple fact that those things are essentially meaningless and narcissistic? Very valid reasons, but there's got to be more to it than that. A social media account is basically a badge of the human species at this point. If you don't have a cyber identity, you're not a real person. I've known people who rarely used social media, but they still had accounts to remain a member of society — even if it was just a Facebook account in their names without a picture or any personal information. So, why has Nick, who is as handsome as hell, decided to not part-take with society? Or, has society asked him to kindly (or not so kindly) step out?

Lost in my thoughts, my bladder almost gives as my phone spasms in my pocket, bringing me back to Earth. Luckily, I'm able to put on my urethra's breaks before losing any liquid. Thank you, Yogi Yolanda, for encouraging me to work my kegels. For the first time since watching Nick's car get swallowed up by the night, I take in my surroundings. I'd been expecting to be close to the coffee place since that's the last place I had a terror-tantrum, and it'd be my sitcom-style luck to have another psychotic episode in front of that poor barista again. Instead, the cracked driveway of my apartment complex, looking like a multi-mouthed monster straight out of a John Carpenter film, is only a few yards ahead.

How had I made it back so quickly?

The quivering in my front pocket continues, so I dig out my phone before the pulsating cancer-magnet gives my bladder any more ideas. The glow of the phone softens the darkness around me as I read the text message:

> **Hey, it's Nick. Thanks for the help and the bathroom banter tonight. I'll try to remember the hacksaws next time. Hope you made it home safely.**
>
> **Sorry about that booty stank...**

CHAPTER 6
ALIEN PULSE

I am succumbing to the inevitable pull of sleep.

My racing mind dissipates into echoing silence as I effortlessly slip through the thin membrane that separates the dreamer from the waking world.

Shedding the mortal coil of my now sleeping body, my mind's eye drifts aimlessly through a fathomless black void with invisible feelers, relentlessly combing the dark dimensionless space with a feverish need to find her.

I know she is in here somewhere.

I unconsciously sift through the countless microscopic fibers and dust particles that occupy my numberless memory banks while searching for something to fill this vast and empty vacuum.

Her sharp, but innocent face.
Her piercing emerald green eyes.
Her crimson waves of red hair.
Her sweet but subtle smell.

Any and all things that could conjure up the tingly, dizzying feelings that tug at the core of my soul whenever she utters my name. Soon, once bits and traces of her are unearthed in augmented piles of decayed memories, a warm pinkish hue absorbs the sterile darkness that envelops me. Replacing the cold denseness with flares of impossibly vibrant multi-colored nebulas, beautiful spectrums of light dance and sway to the mystic rhythms of an ever-expanding cosmos. With my unblinking third eye, I try to configure and assimilate the overwhelming amount of sensory input being mainlined directly to the open nerve endings of my exposed mother-brain. I see each granule cluster of atoms acting as tiny windows into infinite parallel realities where She and I live a perfect life together. The love we share in these worlds radiates with the scorching intensity of a thousand dying suns.

In all of these omnipotent fantasies, I am truly needed. I am truly loved.

I am truly unbroken.

I bask among the celestial globs of flickering images and phosphorescent lights until an alien pulse ripples from outside this heavenly realm and tears a long, seam-like hole in the grand illusionary veil, causing the spectral portals to slowly recede back into the incomprehensible black abyss.

My mind clenches like a fist as I cry out wordlessly for the return of the comforting glow of those borderless windows into nirvana. When my physical eyes finally drift open, I trace the evil sound to the end table where my cell phone is buzzing and shaking around, trying to tell me that I got a text.

Better not be Bobby calling out of work, I think groggily to myself, mildly annoyed, but more so tired. The last time he texted out of work, he told me he broke his leg and had "the green gang disease." I think he meant "gangrene" and probably not the fictional, reptilious villains from the children's cartoon show *The Powerpuff Girls*. I slept all of fifteen minutes before my phone went and thoroughly destroyed my alternate, but somehow more tangible, reality. Squinting my eyes against the blurry backdrop of the screen, I see the text is actually from Harper, and I quickly throw off the covers and turn on the lamp.

> **No prob, Bro-bama. I'll see you tomorrow for more of Bobby-Ray Bitches's Bumpin Beat Block Party.**
> **Don't forget to text me in the morning.**
> **:)**

That primitive emoticon is all it takes to get my

heart racing with a spongy tickle accumulating in my chest as my head spins with the possibilities of what it means under the surface. Does she like me? Does she feel the same warm, open heartedness about me that I do about her? I mean, yeah, I know she likes me as a person, but does she really like me? We are practically identical in almost every way, but that doesn't necessarily mean we are meant to be together. Maybe being sexually repressed is slowly driving me to early onset dementia. Probably all the years of overproduced splooge backing up the pipes and oozing into my porous brain.

Nevertheless, my mind starts to wander back to those spinning windows, and my hands start to drift down the front of my tight, bulging shorts. I revisit these scenarios with my full attention. The scenarios are never the actual act of sex but, rather, the small intricate things leading up to it.

A small tug at the front of my shirt as she pulls me down to passionately kiss me with slightly parted, moist lips.

Her tiny, porcelain hand in mine as we sit on a sandy, shell littered dune facing the roaring sea line as it crashes and crawls across the sparkling wet sand towards our naked feet.

The feeling of my hard fingertips moving across the soft ridges of her navel as she holds my other hand to her breast and purrs longingly into my ear.

Acting on their own, my hands find their way to my part(s) and pull them out in one decisive motion. Barely aware of what I am doing, my hardening grip is met with even more resistance as my blood relocates to my lower body, causing both of them to stand up in proud defiance. Gripping them both now in my hands, I absently-mindedly think how much of a shame it is that I have two impressively nice penises when some people don't even have one. Like a mighty redwood tree split by lightning cast down by God himself. The real irony is that, in this case, getting two for the price of one isn't exactly a great deal. I know most women prefer a big penis, but a combined sixteen inches is more than anyone could ever want or need. With both of them gauging just over eight inches in length and obviously of significant girth, it is a medical marvel that I don't pass out from lack of blood flow to my brain every time I get aroused.

In a semi-conscious state, my weightless arms move my hands up and down the soft curves and shafts of my now rock-hard members. My pulse pounds through from the base to the tips, causing both to swell with the immense pressure being forced onto me by those spinning windows. Each long stroke over my sensitive, velvety head(s) sends waves of ecstasy back to that space, feeding nebulas and strengthening the spiritual intensity. With both hands pumping furiously at uneven tempos to one another, I tense up in anticipation of the big climax.

A tidal wave of dopamine washes over me as pearl white geysers unload from the double-loaded cannons still pulsing and throbbing in my sweaty hands. Luckily, years of having to handle two tigers at the same time has taught me to reflexively aim off to the sides when the big moment comes.

Completely spent and emotionally drained, I get up and clean my mess, take a stiff pee, and fall fast asleep with only lingering thoughts of her.

Chapter 7
The Heart's Manuscript

"Titty sprinkles!"

In my twenties, I still manage to forget that fresh coffee is hot enough to melt asphalt. After the hot cup somehow gyrates in my hand like it's been given a hearty lube job, I'm able to juggle it to the safety of the round table in front of me. Michael Richards would've been proud. To my dismay, my bag looks like the victim of the most powerful post-taco-binge sneeze as a coffee stain soaks into the material. There are worse smells to have lingering around than pumpkin spice. It's the scent of the season, after all.

"Harper, you good?" Megan's voice carries across the deserted coffee shop, tinkling off the shaded windows behind me. About a week after the deranged-coffee-lady incident, I'd decided to stop by the shop after my shift to apologize to Megan for almost making her soil her cute green barista smock. Since then, I've been stopping by regularly. Nick started to give me rides home about two weeks ago, so the stops have been less frequent lately. Megan was usually on duty during the night hours (that douche Damien always fucks up my lattes), and I know how lonely (*scary*) the night can be. She seems to appreciate my Pirate's Tongue, and I appreciate her shrill, feminine laughter. Plus, she can make a mean macchiato.

"The burns are only first degree. I don't think a lawsuit will be necessary." I bat toward Megan with a limp wrist while trying my best to salvage the contents of my now coffee (rhea) colored bag. Thank Christ I had decided to leave *The Man Whose Teeth Were All Exactly Alike* in the safety of my shanty.

Brown napkins in hand, Megan delicately glides across the dining room to help me clean up my mess. Her hands are freshly manicured with a chocolaty varnish that accents her café skin beautifully. Often I tell Megan she's been working here for so long, the melanin in her skin has assimilated to blend in with her surroundings. A cringe-worthy joke, but Megan laughed her designer jean-wearing ass off.

With most of the latte now absorbed into the napkins, I make my way to the trashcan. Before tossing them, I examine the napkins more closely. "Made from recycled paper? Aye dios mio — the progress in our country!" I don't think Megan understands the irony as I animatedly throw the napkins in the trash like I'm throwing away the empty

Oreo packaging left by a roommate, but fuck it.

We sit across from each other at the now clean, but slightly pumpkin-scented, table. Megan crosses her legs and rests her elbows on the table, settling her chin into the arm that has been kept vertical. "Nick have the night off?" After my visits to the shop became less frequent, I'd told Megan it was because I was getting rides with a co-worker. I know what it's like to have people suddenly disappear from your life without reason or warning. I've also done my fair share of disappearing in the past few months and didn't feel like continuing that trend.

I drop my own elbows to the table with far less elegance. "Yup. Just me, Bobby-Ray Bitches, and Las Reinas de Colombia tonight. His nights off are complete shit. Jizz LaQueefa' (*Wiz Khalifa*, for those of you not well-versed in the art of Pothead Poetry...) gets bumped all night like it's a high school graduation party, and the senoras gossip in Spanish all night with their phones in their hands."

The worst part, besides the creepy walk home, was simply that Nick wasn't there. No one to quote Jewish sitcoms to. No one to help me usurp Bobby's stereo with *Jazz From Hell*. No steely blue eyes. No forearms working that mop like powerful pistons. Who knew janitorial duties could be sexy?

I refuse to admit any of this to Megan, but my stupid face must have given some kind of tell because her plum stained lips creep into a knowing smile.

Fuck me...

She drops her eyes to the table as if my heart's

manuscript is written upon it. "So... Nick's pretty cute, right? I mean, he hasn't, like, come into the shop or anything, but I've seen him in his car on the nights that he's stopped with you. He have a girl-friend or anything?" Her caramel (macchiato) eyes lift to meet my green ones, gently insisting for more information. Originally, I'd thought her eyes were much darker. Maybe the primeval part of my mind had darkened my whole world that first week. The summer months in South Harbor had been much colder than those of the fall. But no: her eyes are warm and inviting; they hold a gaze that makes you feel like you're the most important person in the world. If I were given the opportunity to have a lunch date with the president of the United States (even the most attractive and charming, dead or alive — your pick) or Megan, one look into that warm, velvety stare would cause me to say, "Sorry, Mr. President, but I'ma have to pass." Had I been a lesbian or a dude, I'd totally want to bone her. How many hearts has Megan won and broken with this same look?

Picking at my fingernails — trying my best to fake a disinterest — I tell her, "Nah, Nick doesn't have a girlfriend. Well, he's never mentioned one, anyway. Seems like the type of thing that would come up in a discussion. Unless she's a total bitch, I guess."

The topic of relationships and/or significant others had never come up during my conversations with Nick. My first thought was that we had so much other shit to talk about that it just hadn't come up, but lately I'd been wondering how after a month of seeing each other for six or more hours a night, three to six days a week, neither of us had mentioned anything within the realm of relationships. It almost felt like we were both avoiding it, but...

The arm cradling her chin drifts away momentarily to retrieve her phone from beneath her apron. It's the size of paperback novel, and I'll never figure out where Megan can possibly conceal it beneath her snug-fitting clothing that constantly bear hugs her. I'm not sure whether her clothing had fit this tightly when she had purchased it or if the fabric shrunk itself over time just to be more intimate with her skin. Can't say I'd blame it. "What's his last name?" Both of her thumbs are in the ready position for texting and cyber-snooping.

I laugh a little at her adorable attempt to find information. Like she was some hip, sexy Nancy Drew. "He doesn't have any accounts online. No Facebook, no Twitter — not even a Myspace." When Megan had asked me to add her as a friend on Facebook, it'd led to a half-hour long interrogation where Megan tried to get to the bottom of why I was lying to her about not having a cyber presence via any type of profile, and then the questioning sharply shifted to the rationality of not even having Twitter: the laziest form of social interaction known to man. I'm expecting round two of the same locked-doors conversation. Instead, Megan looks up from her phone, puzzled. Her full lips thin slightly as they twitch to the right in a half smirk. She gives me what looks like an almost expectant nod before holstering her cell phone back to its home beneath her apron and then returning to the "head-in-chin" position.

After a pensive pause, Megan lifts her head — ever so delicately — from her chin. She leans back into her seat, folding her arms. The sideways smile tells me she is a little disappointed that I hadn't taken her bait. "Cute guy like that doesn't have a girlfriend? You think he's cute, right?" Our eyes lock in a showdown. She is ever so delicately, but forcibly, picking my locks like the most skilled thief who ever lived. I refuse to break eye contact. Fuck that noise; I'm going to win this Battle of the Bitches. She can't possibly...

...DAMN YOU AND YOUR COMPELLING PEEPERS, MEGAN!

I return her stare, contort my lips into an exaggerated purse, and do my best feminine lisp. "Oh my gawd, he's like, *so* totally dreamy! I *sooo* want to have my babies with him."

Megan doesn't break her gaze, and I know that she's not dropping the subject. I feel like Germany behind Russian lines; I haven't had a girlfriend in so long that my defenses are weak. This is new terrain for me and my tanks are sinking in this snowy landscape around me. No wonder guys get pussy-whipped so easily.

I drop the lisp and allow my face to fall back to its typical positioning. "Alright, fine, he's an attractive man. If I were a bawdy babe, I'd flick my bean to that."

You DID try to do just that, but you are such an utter failure that you can't even masturbate properly. You will die alone without ever experiencing an orgasm.

The crude joke throws Megan off long enough for her to let a few laughs escape. "Okay, so cute guy in a sort-of-city without a girlfriend? He must have his eye on someone, or he's waiting for her." One of her perfectly manicured eyebrows raises briefly at the end of her sentence. This girl is good. But,

I'm determined. And incredibly stubborn.

"Well, I'm sure she's out there somewhere," I say and take a swig of my now tepid latte.

To my surprise, Megan's smile drops. "Come on, Harper. Be a girl with me for just five minutes! I know you have a heart hidden under those black shirts—"

"—I have a sweating problem with my pits—"

"—take a break and be real for a second."

The dart sinks in. Its venom begins to spread, and I succumb to its pull. I can't remember the last time someone had insisted that I be **serious**. All of the people I'd spent the majority of my life with simply assumed that I was incapable of being **serious** and when a **serious** topic did poke its ugly little head up, I frightened it away with my sarcasm. It never took long. Like Michael Richards, I typecasted myself. No one expected anything more of me, and I embraced my role.

I take my phone out of my pocket and place it on the table in front of me. To exemplify this momentary break in character, I lift my stubby index finger above my head and then swandive it against the "Set Timer" button illuminating the finger-smudged screen. I'd say my technique deserved at least the bronze, if I do say so myself. "Alright, five minutes. I warn you, though, I'm not great at this whole having a vagina thing."

In one triumphant grin, Megan looks like she is ten years younger and has just won VIP tickets to a Justin Bieber concert (or whoever the current heart-throb is — damned if I know). Or, I guess she could have been a single twenty-one-year-old who just scored tickets to a Drake concert after a bad breakup and the purchase of the most cleavage-enhancing blouse in existence. Her elbows make their way to the tabletop again, only this time, her hands lay flat on its surface. She leans forward. I can't help but notice how much this movement has perked up her boobs. They're like two orphans pressed up against the toy store on Christmas Eve. It's almost as if the twins want to be in on this juicy gossip, too. "Okay, so you like Nick, don't you?"

My head is already aching from the amount of estrogen in this tiny space. I look up toward the ceiling (is that gum? impressive...) praying that I'm able to get through this conversation without making a poop joke. My eyes drop to Megan's. "He's the most interesting guy I've ever met. We like all of the same shit, and he somehow manages to put up with my awful babbling. He's very sweet and is the definition of eye-candy. Yes, Megan, I like him." There. It was out. Like Ellen DeGeneres (hey, it's not a poop joke).

Megan's smile widens and she glances down at the table briefly, like she's checking for notes, before continuing her interrogation. "Let me ask you a question. Has he tried to fuck you?"

The question completely knocked me on my ass. Not only was the question so unexpectedly bizarre, but "fuck" is not one of Megan's typical vocabulary words. It was like watching a puppy throw a grenade into a children-filled school bus on its way to the Special Olympics. There's silence, and I can feel my eyebrows knitting together in thought as I try my best to process the question. "What did you just ask me??"

It's all I can manage.

"Has he tried to fuck you? Has he tried to bring you to his place, or tried to go into your apartment? Has he accidentally grabbed your ass or boobs? Has he brought up anything sexual? Has he hinted at the idea of having sex at all?"

"No...? Why would you ask me that?" I'm terrible at this language called **Girl Talk**. It isn't my native tongue.

Megan bites her lip briefly in thought. "Cute guy without a girlfriend offers to give you rides home every time you work together? He likes you, Harper."

"Giving a chick a ride home doesn't necessarily mean that he likes her. He could just be **a nice guy**, that's all."

Megan snorts quietly. "Guys will usually only help a girl out if they want something. Most guys want sex, but some of them do nice things because they like the girl. And let's say he is just **a nice guy**. Isn't that even more reason to go for it?"

She has a point there, I must admit.

I tap my half-empty latte cup to break the silence with its hollow hum while I try to think of a response. "Isn't it a little awkward for a girl to ask a guy out? Shouldn't the dude be the one to make the first move with this kind of thing?"

I've got nothing. Nada.

Those caramel eyes roll beneath their lusciously-lashed lids. "Guys can be pretty dense. Some of the nicer ones are a little shy, too. Nick sounds like one of the nicer ones."

"Or, he just wants a friend. I make a better bro than a girlfriend," I say, thinking of past encounters with the opposite sex. I was seen as a homie or a ho. Nothing in-between. Nothing more. I got to go to parties, but it was because I was the one person people could depend on to "tell it like it is." Most of the parties I went to ended with me questioning someone's life choices, or flat-out calling them out on said choices in extreme cases. Normally, this just served as the white stand-up comedian's version of a rap battle; it was uncomfortable enough to be funny, and nobody really won. I was the social assassin, and I was always armed.

She sighs. "Well, Harper, I think you're wrong. You're a pretty girl, you're not fat, you're kind, you're funny... I don't understand why you don't just go for it."

Our five minutes had to be up by now.

"This guy's my manager. If I let him know that I like him and he doesn't feel the same way, there goes my job. That means no more classy dinners of microwaved hot dogs and no more fancy coffee. Nick will make the first move if he likes me, and if not..."

My sentence is cut off by the chiming of the doorbell. The sound makes both of us jump; it's very rare for customers to come in this late. There was one occasion where a couple of local drunkards happened to stumble into the shop, talking about how they liked small titties and pepperoni sticks. I'd politely asked the gentlemen to fuck-off before threatening to call the cops. Other than that exciting occasion, the nights were pretty uneventful.

When I see who dared to enter our coffee shop at this late hour, my heart freezes in my chest:

It's Nick.

Those frosty eyes turn in our direction. Once they settle upon me, he smiles almost bashfully. "Hey, Harper. I was out, and I know you like to stop here sometimes after work. I thought I'd see if you were here and if you'd want a ride home." His hand is behind his head ruffling those luscious locks of his (***seriously***, *Harper*?) (dude's hot; what do you want from me?) as he speaks.

I glance across the table at Megan. She leans back in her chair with a smirk, raising an eyebrow in an "I told you so" gesture.

Fuck you, Megan. **Fuck. You.**

CHAPTER 8
BROKEN HEARTS ARE FOR ASSHOLES

With my hands slick with sweat on the steering wheel and my nerves taut like piano wire, I flick the blinker then turn slowly to merge into the left-hand lane of traffic. The brisk fall air has forced everyone on the windy sidewalks to bundle up against gusts of bone chilling wind that seem to come from all angles out of the whistling night. With the sea blowing in cool, salty air and the monolithic concrete buildings acting as giant stone guides, the city always turns into a gigantic wind tunnel with each change of the season.

I roll up my window against the chill and glance over at Harper quietly sitting in the passenger seat. I hope my showing up at the coffee shop wasn't too weird. I don't want her to think I am a stalker, unless she is into that kind of thing, of course. I only took the night off because Angelica forces me to schedule my vacation time before the end of the year so the company doesn't have to deal with me being out for an entire week.

"So," I finally say after much silence, "how was work tonight? Did you enjoy Mr. Bitches's mixtape selection? I noticed he's been going through a Lil Wayne phase as of late, and by that I mean he can sometimes be seen drinking cough syrup with none of the symptoms of a flu."

Harper giggles and then turns to look out the passenger window where the blurry faces flash by on the dimly lit sidewalk. I notice her demeanor is different tonight. She seems to have a much more serious tone to her that is completely out of the norm. Everything from her voice to the way she absent-mindedly picks at the cuticle of her thumbnail tells me that she is preoccupied somehow. "I brought headphones," she says softly, still looking out the window, "and listened to my own personal mixtapes for most of the night. It wasn't until I had to partner up with him at the end to finish the downstairs break room that I was assaulted with Waka Flocka Flame and Drake. That wasn't even the worst part, though."

"Oh? It gets worse?" I ask as I stop at an intersection to let people use the crosswalk. I quickly steal a glance at her as she teases a loose strand of hair back over her left ear while solemnly watching the crowded street. "He didn't force you to look at his Instagram account, did he?"

"How did you know?!" she yells girlishly, lightly

slapping at my arm as if it were covered in fire ants. Relieved to see her finally lighten up, I also shriek like a twelve-year-old girl at a Chris Brown concert as we pass many confused people on the road. I know she is doing a comedy bit, so I play along like she is severely hurting me.

I futilely flap her hands off my sleeve and say, "He has a thing for taking pictures of himself holding various bottles of fancy liquor and throwing up fake gang signs. I keep telling him that he's going to catch shit for that someday, but he doesn't listen. He just tells me that I don't understand his culture and changes the subject to banging strippers or vaping."

"I notice he has quite the luck with the ladies," she says in between exaggerated yokel chuckling. "I'll never get it. But then again, I can't deny that stupid people need love, too," she jokes.

After several seconds, she adds, "How's your luck with the ladies, Nick?"

The urge to burst out laughing at the very idea of me being anything but a pathetic virgin is so great that, for a second, I literally gasp and then awkwardly pass it off as a sneeze. With no time to think, I say, "Not great," and stonily leave it at that. I can feel her staring at me through the dark mist trying to read my face and posture to see what the real truth is. Those sharp eyes are scanning me, looking for any signs of modesty or deception. I am sure lots of guys play the helpless nerd angle when in actuality they are constantly knee deep in the wading pool of the poon-nami. I know Harper will find out eventually that I am single and will wonder why I don't have a girlfriend or pick up greasy girls from the clubs like some kind of comically sweaty Don Juan. I had months to prepare for this moment, but I never truly accepted the possibility that she was interested in me and now it has come.

So, now I know that she either likes me or wants to know if I am gay. Fantastic.

"I don't mean to be all up in your biz or nothin," she starts to say hesitantly as I make a quick left onto her road without responding. "I just noticed that you never talk about girls and... I'm sorry. You don't have to answer that if you don't want to." She looks away towards the blurry shoulder again and nervously folds her tiny white hands in her lap. Like two sleeping doves.

I know that I have to say something, but I can't tell her the truth. I am four blocks away from her apartment and very close to avoiding the truth if I can get her home before I make even more of an ass clown out of myself. Slowly, I apply pressure to the gas pedal.

After clearing my throat, I say jokingly, "I don't have nearly as much luck as most people since I am kind of a nerd. If only I had that Bobby swagger instead of a bookshelf, then I could find lots of classy ladies, right?"

She sighs deeply at this and then says, "Aside from having to work with that donut puncher, do you know why my night really sucked? It sucked because I spent the whole night missing your nerdy banter. When you aren't there, it's a real drag." She makes an exaggerated sad puppy dog face at me as I turn to see if she is having me on. With her lower lip stuck out and her eyes wide and begging, that look alone would surely make any grown man buckle to his knees. She then places her hand gently on my right leg and says, softly, "You know what I mean, Nick?"

Stunned, I freeze rigidly in my seat. For a split second I feel nothing but the weight of her delicate hand resting on my right leg. The sudden realization that I am speeding in the middle of evening traffic snaps me out of my trance just in time to avoid a black sedan prematurely changing lanes. I swerve back over. With the minor crisis avoided, I lick my cracked lips and say, "Sorry, I didn't see that guy blinker."

Even with the sudden panic of almost getting in an accident, her hand had never left my thigh. I quickly glance down just to make sure that it's real and then look over at Harper. Her eyes are wide and her face upturned to mine in an elegant gesture of hopeful waiting. In the downcast glow of the street-lamps and bright headlights of passing cars, she somehow radiates with a rosy aura that illuminates the dark interior of the car. I almost get sucked into those enchanting emerald eyes silhouetted in a haze of crimson red. I pull myself out again to look at the road.

Nervously, I say, "I... miss work too."

Oh sweet zombie Jesus, what a terrible answer, I immediately think to myself as I tighten my grip on the wheel and curse my feeble brain for having the social graces of a soap dish. I would have been better off accidentally blowing snot everywhere or cutting a loud fart then locking the doors and windows rather than blurting out that know-nothing answer. If only I could have unbuckled my seatbelt and jumped head first out of the driver's side door onto a passing truck heading north towards the interstate after hearing that question, then this whole thing could have been avoided. Not a great way to avoid hard conversation, but then again, anything would have been better than the sloppy mess I had unloaded on myself.

Numbly, I stutter to get another word out before my awful statement can linger too much longer, but she breaks the tension by mumbling, "Yeah. Good thing it's the weekend." Her hand then wilts and slowly floats back to her lap where she sits quietly, her head now turned towards the passenger window. One of the most typical, mundane lines that you could ever utter is not what I wanted to hear come out of her mouth at that moment. I know that to hear those words from Harper is the social equivalent of the person you're calling long distance using a bullhorn to answer the phone. If she had instead told me to "suck a bag of dicks," I would have nothing to worry about.

As I sit coldly and blindly guide the car over to the curb in front of Harper's apartment, I mentally fumble through my "Bobby Folder," desperately searching for something funny or clever to say to make up for my enormous fuck-up. How could I have missed a clear opportunity to make a move on her without fear of total rejection? She just told me that she missed me, and my reaction is, "Blah Blah I'm a dumbass."

It is confirmed. I will die alone.

As I limply sit in front of her apartment listening to the motor idle, waiting for the sound of the passenger door to open and close with no word of goodbye, I can't help but stare blankly at the steering wheel and hate myself for being so useless. As I am about to lift my head to say goodnight, I feel her hand slip into mine. I turn my gaze toward hers. As I do, she bends over the center console and tenderly kisses my right cheek before I have time to speak. The kiss has the mental impact of a sucker punch to the jaw, and for five seconds I see nothing but stars and fireworks in front of my eyes. After the overwhelming religious-like experience starts to fade and my tunnel of sight widens, I feel her hand leave mine and the distant words, "Goodnight, Fag. Thanks for the lift," come echoing out of the distant silver specks, showering confetti-like across the entire world around me.

I sat at the curb for nearly fifteen minutes trying to figure out whether I should grow a pair and go up to her apartment or slink back home. I always heard that women love when men are spontaneous, adding a much-needed romantic spin to the mix. Surely this would be the perfect moment to show her how I really feel and throw away my insecurities. I could buzz her and ask to come up to her place with something really important to say. It can't wait until tomorrow. Once upstairs, I would profess my undying love for her and accept whatever grievances may come. Damned or not, this is the time to act.

So, like a true man of love, I packed up my balls and drove home alone. Later, I jacked off twice(x2) before falling into a very deep, guilt infested sleep.

Proving once again that, without a doubt, broken hearts are for assholes.

Chapter 9
A Cake Without Eggs

The walk to my apartment feels like taking a dump in a public restroom; you *know* the person washing her hands at the sink knows what you're up to in your stall, but once the shit starts to fall, there really is no going back. It only continues to fall endlessly, stinking up the room for everyone with the misfortune of being there. Kissing Nick was the biggest porcelain-shattering fart I could've let slip by my clenched sphincter. The hand on the thigh was innocent enough — I *could* have coughed to cover that one — but there's no going back from that raunchy, juicy trouser trumpet that I just let rip in the car. What the hell was I thinking?

You were thinking that you like this guy, and for once you expressed how you really feel without cracking (oy, that toilet analogy...) a joke or being sarcastic. Plus, your suspicions of Nick liking you were validated by Megan: the most feminine, perceptive woman you've ever met. He's the one who stopped by to pick you up, anyway. Isn't that a "move" in itself?

Luckily, my apartment is on the first floor. This means that there isn't the awkward too-rushed-to-be-sexy saunter up a flight of stairs, and I don't have to face Nick again before dashing to the safety of my apartment (which I wouldn't have done even in the most extreme of circumstances; I would've walked up them bitches backwards to avoid any post-kiss eye contact). I say a silent prayer as I miraculously unlock my door without fumbling my keys to the pavement. With the skill of a woman who has played out every possible "chase" scenario in her mind, I:

> *(you really should stop watching all of those serial killer documentaries)*
> (but they keep me on my toes!)

open the door; dart into the doorway like a dog that's just been sprayed by a skunk; swing the door behind me; force it closed with my ass; and lock the deadbolt in one fluid movement. The "rustic" ambiance of this place demands that the door be too swollen for the frame, so the extra muscle is necessary to push the deadbolt into place. The extra toosh-thrusting isn't just me being overly dramatic (cowardly). Within the first two nights at my new crib, I had my deadbolt technique down *TIGHT*. I'm prepared for the speediest assailant, clown with a chainsaw, bill collector, or cliché zombie (how ironic it would be for all of those zombie fan-girls to have their freaky-fetish fantasies come true...).

All this time, even as I'm in survival mode, I wonder what Nick is thinking about while he sits in his car. The warmth of his textured, unshaven cheek still lingers on my lips as I lean against the door. I wasn't sure what to expect. Nick's composure after I asked the question about the ladies seemed to suggest that he either had a shitty experience with a woman, or he has never *had* any experience with a woman. How in the Blue-Fuck does a man that attractive *not* have women crawling after him like sexually deprived sirens? Was he *fucking* with me? Was his reaction some sort of defense mechanism?

You know all about defense mechanisms...

I do a James Bond-esc half roll to the left of the door, settling my stomach and the palms of my hands on the neighboring wall so I can peek out from the old pillowcase that serves as my privacy curtain (I keep it classy). Headlights still shine from the buckling driveway. Nick is still here. Is he going to try to come in? A more likely scenario is that he's calling Angelica **right now** to request that she fire the foul-mouthed new girl or to give his resignation as a means of avoiding ever having to be in my presence again after this horrid encounter...

Are you prepared for the possibility that he MIGHT try to come into your apartment?

...the thought had never occurred to me that Nick might take that small act of affection as an invitation to the Pants Party. He didn't seem like the type of guy to put a banana in the fruit salad of a person he pretty much just met, but past experiences have proven to me time and time again that most guys who are even mildly interested in me only want to check their oil. Once they find out that I'm more sexually awkward than a nun at a Chippendales, the "friendship" ultimately ends. Maybe I'm the lamest lady in her twenties ever, but shoving a body part into the body part of another person seems like a pretty big fucking deal. **SOMEONE IS LITERALLY INSIDE OF YOU!** It's not like he's just shaking your hand. By the time some of my former friends turned twenty, the number of people they had *fickte* was a number larger than their own ages. Despicable — disgusting. Okay, maybe I'm being just a *teensy* bit uptight and judgmental... but, that's just me.

Literally, that's. Just. Me.

Aren't you being a little bit hypocritical about the whole sex thing? It's not like you haven't played Hide the Cannoli a time or two.

Sure have. They were the most unsatisfying experiences of my life. I think I would rather have my tartar scraped at the dentist's office while being forced to watch *Footloose* with my eyes pried open and with sound enhancing hearing aids crammed into my ear canals. The first batter up was a mess — a Goddamn mess. It was like getting a haircut from someone fresh out of beauty school. You sit down in that nice, cozy chair and make yourself comfortable. The girl (dude) takes a little too long (yeah, he wishes...) to make that first cut. She starts to cut, you begin to relax... until you look up in the mirror and notice that she has cut five inches more of your hair than you'd requested. This is *nothing* like you'd expected. You stare in shock and dismay at the freakshow that is now your hair; you can see the discarded remains of what were once your beautiful locks gaping up at you from the floor below. **Why Harper, *WHY* did you think this would be a good idea!?** At that point, all you can do is hope for the best and just allow her (him) to finish the job without a tip. Needless to say, batter out.

Then comes another contender. Swing and a miss. Swing... and a miss. Somehow hits the fucking ball backwards, *BACKWARDS* — and busts someone's windshield. Aaaandd... he's out.

At that point, I threw my hands up in defeat and tossed in my cleats. I pretty much accepted the fact that sex "wasn't my thing" and that my ovaries would shrivel to raisins by the time I turned thirty due to the lack of stimulation.

Thinking about it, there was one key ingredient missing from the failed sexscapades of my past: love. Was this whole sex thing like baking a cake? Are all ingredients needed in order to produce an edible result? Yeah, I have the sugar, and someone brings some flour to the mix, but without the eggs, that shit is just going to fall apart and become a putrid, inedible mess. Is love the binding agent I've been missing?

If this is the case, the bakery will have to be closed until those figurative hens start laying.

Stop with the stupid fucking metaphors and fo-

cus! You might have done fucked up, Harper. You kissed him, sort of, so he knows you like him. There is no turning back from that. This isn't France where a kiss on the cheek is proper practice among friends. This is America: home of impersonal interactions and the suppressing of emotions. Any physical contact will be taken as a sexual invitation.

I think of Megan's words in the coffee shop.

"Guys can be pretty dense. Some of the nicer ones are a little shy, too. Nick sounds like one of the nicer ones."

A nice guy.

Please, for the love of all things holy, be one of the nicer ones, Nick. Be **a nice guy.** Please don't take my poorly thought out attempt at being flirtatious as an admission ticket to the slip-and-slide.

As if on cue, I'm brought back to the reality of my shitty apartment by the sound of tires on broken pavement. Never have I heard a more beautiful sound in my life. It's like the soothing sounds of waves crashing against a sandy, shell scattered beach. Just to be sure that what I'm hearing is for real, I turn ever so slightly to peer out from the curtain (*it's a goddamned spit-stained pillowcase and you know it*) and watch the headlights of Nick's car slowly fade out of existence.

I'll be damned. He is one of the nice ones:
A nice guy.

There might be a chance.

CHAPTER 10
REVERSE SEXUAL HARASS-MENT IN THE WORKPLACE

I had spent the entire weekend worrying and hypothesizing how work was going to be now that I know Harper has feelings for me. Well, she *did*, anyway. If my little mental disappearing act didn't thoroughly convince her that I was the next Norman Bates, then *maybe* she still likes me. I contemplated for days about sending her a funny or random text like I usually do. I decided against it once I forced myself to think about anything but her for two seconds. How could I have been so incredibly spineless? Her straightforwardness and guarded posture alone should have told me that she was trying to convey a serious demeanor for once, and I joked my ass off at everything she had to say. I bet subconsciously I knew that she liked me, and somehow, I sabotaged myself to avoid having to be a man. It's a wonder that

I don't slide around on my belly like a mud-covered seal everywhere I go. I am so spineless that I should probably just go live at the bottom of the ocean with the rest of the sexless jellyfish, living out of sunken ships and eating coral reef like some kind of fleshy, pronged version of SpongeBob.

I had no choice but to sit and wait for Monday night and pray to Jeebus that she didn't hate me for being so dense.

When I pull up to the job, I see everyone's vehicles parked in a loose circle around a small graffiti tagged parking lot by the edge of the building. A huge glass slab juxtaposed against the distant orange glow of the inner city, the sheer size of it made me feel miniscule. Massless. As I near the spray-painted grid at the foot of the colossus, I start to panic. With the night setting in fast, I recklessly veer past silent parked cars and clumsily pull into a spot, eager to get started before Harper got there on foot. I nervously get out of the car and unlock the back doors. As I lean into the backseat to pick up the mop buckets, I hear the crackling of dry leaves coming from the thick row of dying brown hedges to my right. A rough voice from directly behind me says, "You basting those turkeys?" in a terrible Russian (or Japanese?) accent. I have the terrifying realization for a moment that I might have to pull sausage(s) to scare this guy just long enough for me to defend myself.

Hey...they have to be good for *something*.

My initial frightened confusion quickly turns to rage as I feel a hard slap on my left ass cheek. Waves of primal, impulsive fear surge through my body, and I fly into action. Reflexively, I bolt straight up as if I were trying to jump through the sunroof to safety. I bop the top of my head hard on the roof interior, probably putting another nice-sized dent in my already crater filled car. Still in anti-rape mode, I twirl around, fists raised, expecting to have to fight some crazed rapist loose from the mental hospital or possibly Bobby drunk at work again, but I instead see Harper. Her sly smile and elegant glowing face loom out of the dim haze of the street light pollution and decrepit shrubbery. My clenched fists slowly loosen, and I force out a laugh as I rub reflexively at the soon to be throbbing lump on the top of my noggin.

"Hey, Nick," she says in between childish fits of laughter. "I'm sorry, I couldn't resist. Need some help?" She reaches out for the collection of littered buckets near my feet.

I clumsily pick them up off the pavement and hand them to her. Almost inaudibly, I say, "Oh...Thanks," and duck back into the car to pretend to busy myself with categorizing various soap and bleach containers before I hear her wading through the scattered piles of dead leaves to the front of the building to join the others.

Off to a great start, I cynically think to myself as I pull out a box full of rags and set it on the trunk lid. At the rate I'm going, I will probably end up shunning her into quitting. I can't say that I don't understand her confusion to my weirdness around her now, but I really don't know what to do. I mean, the simple fact that I can't explain to her how I really feel makes everything that much more complicated. I know dating is out of the question, but there has to be a way for a man(?) and a woman to be close friends without greasing the pan. I can't let a simple misunderstanding like my inability to toss woo let a perfectly good friendship wither and die. The way I figure, if I can still salvage the friendship, then everything will be ok.

And besides, it's literally the only option I have left.

I need to talk to her about what happened and clear the air so we can maybe salvage the awesome bro-ship we had. I can kick myself for the rest of my life for not trying to flirt back. In the end, Logic always rules. Flirting would've led to kissing, kissing would've led to groping, groping would've led to undressing, and undressing would've led to shaming.

As the old mantra goes: what would be the point?

Starting the nightly ritual, I unlock the lobby doors, help load up the carts, and assign everyone a check sheet and area of the building to start on first. Even though the building has over thirty floors, each three to four belonging to a separate business or legal branch, we are only responsible for the first three.

With Bobby and Luciana on the third floor and Harper and Sophia on the second floor working separate corners, I am left in the main lobby, alone, struggling with some ancient pre-chewed gum that I found on the bottom of the receptionists' main desk. As I am scraping gum that has a striking resemblance to the dog from Frasier next to what looks like dried clumps of tapioca pudding, I can't stop thinking about how I am going to talk to Harper. How does one tell the woman of his dreams to politely piss off? If she does in fact still like me, then she definitely won't once I break the news to her that I am undateable. It's a nice white lie for everyone to enjoy.

You ask, "How are you undateable?"
I say, "Smell my finger."

It is a crude but effective technique. Over the years I have learned to always deal with these uncomfortable situations by means of diversion and bad jokes. It doesn't always work in the way of sparing anyone's feelings, but I get to avoid embarrassing myself with tales of my freak show fun sticks.

Not wanting to wait any longer, I decide that the time is now. I toss down my scraper, abandoning the other half of Eddie's gross portrait, and start for the second floor. As I am about to walk through the entrance to the stairs, Harper comes flying out of the doorway and almost slams face first into my chest. I reach out to catch her just as the door swings back and knocks her squarely in the shoulder. For the few seconds that our skins touch, my electric fingertips meld to her lush pigment. My constitution slightly wavers at this divine feeling she radiates, but once again logic prevails. I take a deep breath and dive in feet first.

"Harper, I need to talk to you about…"

"Oh my god, Nick!" she blurts out once she catches her breath. "You have to see this. Come with me." She then grabs my hands with painted claws and starts to drag me to the staircase heading up to the second floor.

"Oh, shit," I say while she pulls and tugs me up the towering stairs, "Sophia isn't dead, is she?"

She laughs maniacally at first, but then anxiously says, "No, Jagoff. Just shut up and follow me." She breaks her hold from me to jog up the edged slab of stairs, sending her tiny childlike steps echoing through the dizzyingly high staircase. Looking up briefly to see where it ended, I get a case of the spins and have to force myself to look away just to keep up with Harper's pace.

We climb the endless stairs until coming to a big metal door with 3rd floor spray painted in red on the front, and when I try to ask again what this is all about, she spins around and lays a small white finger across my lips; another reminder for me to shut my face. I have absolutely no idea what is going on, but I am in too deep now to turn back.

Slowly, Harper pulls the door open and gestures at me to follow her in. Squatting with our backs to the wall, we creep down the sides of a long, dark corridor of offices and cubicles. From high cubicle dividers and office desks, Garfield plush toys and Dilbert calendars loom over us in the bleeding light like gargoyles and bell towers in an ancient gothic city. Feeling like I am in a special ops unit, I duck and weave past chairs and copiers as if at any moment I could lose my life in this lawless jungle of binders and fancy office swivel chairs. As we near the end of the hall, I notice the sound of music amplifying from somewhere beyond one of the distant corners. Once at the end of the hall, I instantly recognize the music that I am hearing. Well, technically it's not music, but for all intents and purposes, that is what society deems it as.

I am talking, of course, about the warbly, nonsensical sounds of Future.

Harper stands in front of me just at the mouth of the right-hand corner. Hands bracing the walls for stability, her pink lips mouth the words, *"Get down."* She mimes to look around the lighted corner with caution, and then she slowly looks out herself. Taking a different angle than her, I carefully edge my way to the very end of the wall and stick my head out into the light.

There, at the end of the adjacent hallway, is Bobby with his boombox standing in front of a full-length mirror that some reckless bastard had decided to fix to the front of his office door. Had that reckless bastard accounted for this exact situation, this tragedy might have been avoided.

Facing the mirror with his back to us, it is pretty obvious — even at a distance — that Bobby is using the mirror to take shirtless selfies of himself as he dances to Future. His flakey, jaundice yellow skin shimmers and wanes in the hum of the overhead fluorescent lighting, reminding me vaguely of the pale, shriveled frogs that I would find hiding under large, flat rocks down by the riverfront as a kid. The top of his spine is knotted and tense, nubs and bumps protruding here and there, disorganized against the natural curvature of his back. Even his arms, long stick-like birch branches wrapped with raw pizza dough, have an odd, uneven shape to them. I can make out vague tattoos (a shaky doodle of a handicap sign smoking a bong on his upper right shoulder), but what really captures my imagination is the way he is dancing for the camera. Flexing his imaginary muscles as he pumps his fists and gyrates his hips in front of the reflective slab, Bobby resembles more of a misshapen toad marionette than the sexy rap star he undoubtedly sees himself as. I often wonder how he gets laid so consistently, and this just further deepens the mystery. His greasy backside glistens and perspires as he works his odd magic for future Tinder dates. In the mirror's reflection, I can see him trying desperately to squeeze his gelatinous midsection into a set of passable abs, but failing miserably.

Oh well, I am sure they have an app for that.

After giving up on his six-pack, he walks over to his cart and grabs a spray bottle. He glances at the label for only a second before spritzing the chemicals onto his chest. His crooked, boney hands pump limply on their own accord to fat beats and auto-tuned mumbling as the mystery mist slowly trickles down on him. While the improvised body oil was probably just window cleaner, I can't help but wonder if maybe he grabbed bleach by mistake. It would certainly account for the lack of skin tone and red, scaly surface in some areas of his chest and stomach.

It takes every ounce of self-discipline to keep myself from bursting out into hysterical laughter. Judging by the look on Harper's face, she is also having the same internal struggle. We choke and muffle our snickering until suddenly Bobby twirls around in our direction.

Before hurtling back into the dark hallway, I catch a quick glimpse of his dark, splotchy nipples hanging loosely on his pasty, sunken chest. They resemble slightly melted milk duds that someone had let roll around in their front pocket. I wonder if the window cleaner (or bleach) is actually causing them to smear. His hypnotic jiggling and those silly nipples are almost my undoing. I thought for sure he saw us spying and was coming down to give us hell. Instead, he walks briskly into an open office somewhere just before reaching our position. Confused, I slowly poke my head back around the corner to see what he is up to.

Back at the mirror now, I can see that he has

something red and shiny in his right hand. With his free hand, he unzips his pants. By the time I realize that he had taken someone's stapler out of the side office, it is too late. The stapler disappears down the front of his pants. With a few minor adjustments, it is now a prop in Bobby's photo shoot. He continues to work the camera with his newfound bulge, adjusting the stapler here and there to get the best shot of his "package." I honestly think he would be better off with a stapler for a cock, actually. Aside from avoiding the numerous child support payments and trips to the VD clinic, he would be an instant hit at late night office parties.

Harper and I simultaneously gawk at each other in disbelief before scampering back down the hall to the entrance for the stairs. Once back on the staircase, we quickly shut the door and proceed to lose our heads laughing and mimicking Bobby's sexy polish sausage dance. With tears rolling down our cheeks and hot stitches forming in our sides, we sit together on the first step down and let the hilarity run its course.

"I'm sorry," Harper says after nearly falling head first down the flight of stairs while nursing her splitting sides. "I came up here after finishing the second-floor bathroom to see what he had left, and I found him like that. Good thing I have an irrational fear of elevators, or he might have heard me coming." She continues to giggle. Once the fit passes, she turns and asks me earnestly, "What were you saying before I pulled you up here? I hope it wasn't anything important." Her face grows stern as she waits for my response.

Not wanting to ruin the moment we just shared with apologies and excuses for my behavior last Friday, I say, "I just wanted to know if you needed a ride home tonight after the shift. That's all," while trying my hardest to shield my true intentions from her scrupulous stare.

"Oh, sure," she says with just a hint of suspicion in her voice. She then adds, "You sure that's what you had to urgently talk to me about?" Her faint smile tries to hide the transferred tension passing between us, but faint lines of worry show through. Like two magnets of the same polarity, our growing emotional closeness threatens to repel us farther apart. An invisible hardness that only becomes stronger with each new lie and procrastination.

I fight the maddening urge to confess and quickly push it aside and say, "Yeah, I wouldn't make a lady walk home in a city infested with dancing, hairless albino monkeys with staplers stashed in their banana hammocks. It is brutal, I know; I have been to the gates of madness."

After sharing another hearty laugh session at Bobby's expense, we descend the stairs to the second floor to gather up Harper's supplies and to see how Sophia is doing on the other side of the building.

For the rest of the night, Harper and I talked and joked with each other like usual. For the first time in days, I felt relaxed. After knowing that the drama I had thought I would be walking into at the beginning of my shift was all in my head, I could finally start to put that awkward night behind me and enjoy the friendship. Of course I still have feelings for her and probably always will, but logic dictates the future for me in a blessing of self-security and a curse of unavoidable loneliness. No matter what, she will reject me. Whether it's two weeks from now or twenty-five years from now, she will find out that I am a broken shell of a real man and leave. Instead of going for broke, I will settle with friendship. Not to play down how much I appreciate her as a friend; I just know that our love will forever remain in the void. Trapped behind those spinning windows for all eternity while I toil away at a life that is barely worth living alone.

Even as I am dropping her off in front of her apartment, I wonder what would happen if I leaned over and kissed her just as she kissed me before. The side of me that begs me to seek out others and make real connections is always overshadowed by the bombastic tenor of voices telling me that I will only end up where I started.

Alone and full of shame for something that I can't control.

I look into her bright emerald eyes and fantasize about making a move. I predictably end up just saying goodnight and regretfully watch her step out onto the curb. As Harper walks up the sidewalk to her apartment, she stops just before the doors. She turns around to mime the wormy native dance of the indigenous lizard people of South Harbor to me, using her tiny gloved hands to represent Bobby's misshapen mocha nipples, before prancing off towards her place. I can't help but sit at the curb and wonder how cruel life is for sending someone so perfect my way knowing that I could never really be with her.

At times of overwhelming self-doubt like this, I often think about seeing a doctor and getting some kind of intensive surgery to get one of them removed. I know I could never go through with it. As much as I don't like certain aspects of myself, I know that lopping off one of my thunder sticks won't fix anything. Whether I want to accept it or not, these two meat swords are a part of who I am as an individual. I bitch and cry about having two dicks when in the reality outside my tiny, self-absorbed bubble, there are people walking around with two heads or no face who have perfectly fine relationships with other "normal" people. I blame my problems on the twins, but deep down I know that I scapegoat them for my own emotional shortcomings. In a lot of ways, it is easier and much less painful to avoid love and relationships. My usual game plan is anytime an opportunity comes my way, I throw up my hands and secretly play the deformity card.

Not my fault; this is just the way God made me.

Chapter 11
The Importance of Being Thoreau

I never fully understood just how much control a tiny computer had over my life until I cut it out completely. Until I cut the cord, so to speak.

(See what I did there??)

You know, before moving to South Harbor, I never really thought about how awful it must be to live alone. For the majority of my life, I've been surrounded by people. Of course, there were times when I had the house to myself. It's not like I was never alone, but there was always evidence of human existence. A dish I didn't dirty crusting on the counter. A half-empty, MGS stained container of chicken Lo Mein that took every ounce of my self-control not to eat. Now that I'm living on my own, this lack of people-presence is overwhelming. A five-day-old food-hardened plate would be even more beautiful than anything Van Gogh ever shat out. I used to beg for some privacy and silence, but now I dream of smelling the farts of another human being.

To further enhance my point, a thump reverberates off of the empty walls when I set my coffee cup on the counter. The loneliest applause known to man (and woman — you get what I mean). Carefully, I turn it by the handle so it's at an angle where I won't lacerate my lip off the chip kissing its rim. I'd hate to get blood in my name brand, top-shelf instant coffee.

(I bet if you'd just stop going to Starbucks, you could save up enough money in a month to buy a coffee maker.)

(Fuck you; I'm an American.)

The sandy scraping this causes is so obnoxiously loud, I feel like I'm stuck in the middle of a post-apocalyptic film by Stanley Kubrick. At least I know I don't have mice. I'd hear them breathing and screwing in this vacuum.

Sipping a cup of coffee, even instant coffee, at your kitchen counter on a chilly day off sounds so wholesome, right? An optimist could argue that I might adopt this positive outlook if I perhaps, *maybe*, **possibly**, had some sort of stool or something to sit on. Somehow, I doubt that. The cold wood against my ass would only make the day seem colder.

It's Sunday. My day off. My day cut off from society completely. Fall is now in full balls-out mode, and the cold leaks into my apartment through every available crevice of this place. I don't even have a freakin' couch to burrow myself into. I totally get why solitary confinement is a punishment in prison. I'm even considering beginning some sort of stupid petitioned cause to put an end to this cruel, inhumane punishment within our prison system. No one should be subjected to this breed of torture. Well, maybe kid diddlers... All I'm able to do is sit alone in this hole of mine and wait for tomorrow to come.

I bring my cup of tepid, microwaved coffee to my lips, secretly hoping that it'll taste *so* bad that my mind won't be able to focus on anything other than the perplexing answer to how in the fuck anyone could make a cup of coffee taste like a double yeast infection.

Shit...
It's only a Dirty Dishwasher level of disgusting.

Coffee in tow, I scuff my horribly mismatched slippers over my scruffy carpet (that sounds like slang for old lady fetish porn...). Never in my life have I wanted a chair so badly. If the Tooth Fairy were real, I would yank out every tooth in my head in trade for just one kitchen chair. With my bare hands. Even one of those non-padded chairs that make your back scream like a bitch if you dare spend more than twenty minutes in it. Not wanting to spend more time than necessary in my poor excuse for a bed, I turn and let my back lean against the wall behind me.

I literally have nothing to do. Yes, I know what

the word "literally" actually means, too. I *literally* know the definition. I quickly scan the pile of books by my "bed." I've read them all. Even if I hadn't, I'm not sure whether I'm feeling the whole reading thing today. Yeah, I have a library card and do read quite frequently, but books h'ain't no good. After a period of time, anyway. Reading isn't a shameful, pointless activity or anything, but books h'ain't people. I now completely understand why so many people in their twenties decide to find a roommate. I used to assume that it was due to lack of finances, or maybe it was in the hopes of landing a cutie of the opposite sex (or same sex if that's what you're into — I don't judge). Now, I think it's more about avoiding the crushing loneliness that comes with the single life.

When I sit down (*How the fuck can you do that? You have no chairs!*) and force myself to think about it, these past couple of months have been the only time in my life that I've been truly alone. I mean, for realz, Boo Radley (the creepy neighbor dude from *To Kill a Mockingbird*, for all you non-readers) alone. Before I pulled my little disappearing act, I had the option of mindlessly exploring the Internet and social media accounts to fill that void. With my accounts all closed and no Internet service, this is no longer an option. Shutting the world out from myself also shut myself out from the world.

Oh, woe is me.

MUSIC CUE: *Radiohead*

You have more DVDs than some people have brain cells. Stop being a whiney bitch and watch your John Carpenter collection.

Who wants to binge watch horror movies while snuggling into a heap of blankets on the fucking floor? That's bullshit. Bullshit, I tell you. Watching horror movies is an absolute impossibility for me while I'm alone, anyway. So, I guess I'll never watch another scary movie again. I could put on some mildly presentable clothing, call an Uber, and treat myself to a little retail therapy... oh wait, I HAVE NO MONEY! I've heard of having a day of rest, but this is just ri-goddamn-diculous.

Suddenly, my phone is in my hand. Yes, it happened **suddenly**. When had I even taken the thing out of my pocket? The glowing screen stares up at me, mocking me with its glossy, fingerprint smudged screen. I haven't been able to find a wireless connection in months, so having a smartphone has basically become pointless. Not very smart of me, eh? Yeah, I text Nick from time to time (*you'd be texting him now if you weren't such a wet pussy...*), but one of those cheap brick phones could accomplish that without having to pay for a data plan.

...wait.

A data plan?

A data plan.

Oh my sweet, succulent Jesus — A DATA PLAN!!

You dumb fuck. You completely forget that your phone bill includes data for your phone, didn't you?

Jesus Butt-Fucking Christ...

I'd been so paranoid of going over my allotment that I turned off the mobile data on my phone. My bank account had fallen into the negative integers, bashing its head off of every pasta and bread purchase I'd reluctantly made. I wasn't going to risk an inflated phone bill. No sir. No way. No how. Now that I've been working, my bank account has finally been able to rise back onto its feet, cleaning all of the blood and regret from its tattered remains, and we both began to put on some weight. I mean, going online for just a few minutes wouldn't chomp up all of my data, right? There'd be no harm in checking out the news online or taking a quick peek at my email.

My fingers tap in the passcode and skim across the cool screen until the grey settings icon stares back at me. All it would take is a few taps and swipes, a few email activation links...

My index finger hovers above the grey, circular gear. Its teeth grin back menacingly. The light illuminates it in anticipation. Am I shaking right now? I've heard of Internet addiction, but I have to admit that I was unaware of the post-heroin addiction tremors. Can a person seriously jones for Internet access?

*But, do you **really** want to subject yourself to that? Think about all of the questions? The phony sentiments?*

It's true. As soon as my account becomes active again, the questions/comments would flood in.

Harper, where have you been? Harper, what happened to you? Harper, why didn't you say goodbye? Harper, Harper, **HarperHarperHarper**. It's nauseating just thinking about the fake expressions of care. But, there's the alternate, and worse, possibility.

> *No one will say shit.*
> *No one noticed you left.*
> *No one fucking cares.*

As annoying as the relentless comments would be, it'd be even worse to re-enter the unicorn-rainbow-fluffy world of social media only to find that your absence wasn't even noticed. With my luck, I'd login to my accounts with a stupid, shit-eating grin on my face only to find no alerts. No messages. Nada. Maybe that old expression about ignorance being bliss is true in this **situation**. I drop my head back against the wall and try to process.

Okay, so you're bored and alone. That's inevitable when you decide to just take off and begin a new life. The loneliness is beginning to crush your poor, shrunken spirits. Of course it is. Humans are social animals by nature. Why do you think organizations as stupid and pointless as Frat and Sorority Houses can even exist? No one wants to be alone. But that doesn't mean you should just throw your hands up and seek out false socialization. The Internet, as comforting as it is, is not authentic companionship. It isn't the Internet you are jonesing for. It's human contact. You're better off reading some sappy romance novel from the library than reconnecting to social media. Do you really think a few "I miss you" comments or some cute puppy videos are going to fulfill that void? Nope. And if they do, it would be temporary. Leave it be.

Glancing at the hunk of metal (and whatever else a phone is made of these days) again, I drop my hand to my side. My knuckles thud against the wall painfully. The abomination is no longer in my view. It doesn't take long for me to realize that reactivating my accounts would make all of this moving and "finding myself" bullshit for nothing. Even a quick peek into my email inbox or Yahoo News would be a bad idea. Yeah, being alone sucks, but at least I'm forced to **think**.

I'm not distracting myself from what my life really is. Being surrounded by people all of the time makes it impossible to meditate on what's really important in life, because there's always some asshole around to appease. Having a cellphone only further mucks up the whole idea of becoming an intellectual; the possibility of someone interrupting your life is a constant. I mean, Thoreau spent over two years living out in the wilderness so he wouldn't be bothered. I'm in no way, shape, or form as badass as H.D. Thoreau. I'd surely die if I walked my ass out to the woods in an attempt to be self-sufficient.

You know what else Thoreau had over you? He had chairs.

I raise my arm and look down. I gaze back up at myself from the glossy blackness. I decide to compromise. With one push of my finger, I disappear and am replaced by blinding light. I tap the contacts icon and find Nick. It doesn't take long, considering I only have three numbers in it, the other two being Angelica from Mona's Cleaners and the Greek House of Pizza two blocks away. I type quickly so I don't have time to question my actions and puss out. The tappa-tappa-tappa of my typing resonates off of the empty, peeling walls just like the coffee mug's thudding had.

Hey Fag-a-tron, does it always get this fuckin cold in the fall here? My frostbitten tits are about to break off...

He's not going to reply, but what the hell. I don't have anything else going on. I tuck my phone back into the safety of the pocket of my sweatpants and try to forget about it. I've set out my chair. All I can do now is wait.

As I'm about to make my way back to the kitchen (nice that it's only a matter of turning around...) to microwave my already cold coffee, I feel a tickle on my right thigh. I dig my phone back out and see the illuminated screen:

When it happens, you could donate your nipples to Bobby. I think his are broken.

CHAPTER 12
CITY OF FREAKS

Without a doubt, my favorite holiday to celebrate is Halloween. Every year since I was four, I have been dressing up in ill-fitting costumes to trick or treat with all the other free spirits of the night, searching for free candy and avoiding the houses with fruit and toothpaste for all of those foolish enough to inquire. I have long since grown out of my days of vandalism and candy binges, but every year I lazily pick out some kind of costume, which for the past five years has been Wayne Gretzky (nothing but my street clothes and an old hockey mask) and walk around the city with total anonymity.

Even as a kid, the thrill of roving around in familiar settings surrounded by tiny demons and monsters high on glucose, and sometimes other chemicals, was enthralling. Through the narrow slits or floppy eye-holes, I could hold my head high and walk freely knowing that no one could separate me from the others. I was just another freak among countless droves of freaks roaming the streets with no prejudice, only a lust for sweet things.

Unlike Christmas or arbitrary fake holidays like Valentine's Day or Father's Day, Halloween holds a special narcissistic quality without nearly the amount of family participation. I love my Mom and I know she loves me, but Christmas and the other family function holidays always felt sad and forced when I was younger. I never expected Mom to buy me a hundred toys to make up for Dad leaving, and she never did. The gifts were secondary to the fact that my Dad bailed on us when we needed him most. Christmas only serves as a yearly reminder of poor decisions made far too long ago to be reversed.

This year, I am lucky enough to share this love of Halloween with Harper, who — in fact — loves all things dark and scary even more than I do. When I semi-casually brought up a costumed stroll of the city together, already expecting her to have made plans elsewhere, she practically tore my arm off in excitement to go. I told her about my lame Wayne Gretzky costume, but she refused to tell me what she had planned for hers. We made plans to meet in front of her apartment around sundown that night. Donning my mask (I should really start saying that I'm Jason Voorhees since Gretzky didn't play goalie) and my festive black hoodie depicting a cartoon Gallagher taking a dump into the open top of an angry jack-o-lantern, I drive over to Harper's place and wait on the sidewalk.

When she finally comes out, I barely recognize her. I do a double take at the bizarre creature walking towards me out of the dull paint-splotched door. Her costume consists of nothing but her regular clothes and hideous movie style makeup that, upon first glance, is frighteningly realistic. Her lips are torn off and both her eye sockets excrete thick, dark lines of purplish blood. Her pupils are jet black and a huge pulpy gash along her right cheek exposes a bright pink jawline and yellowing teeth. I feel sick at first looking at it, but once she comes closer, I can still see how beautiful she is underneath the appearance of a mangled corpse and my stomach relaxes.

I start to feel stupid for not putting more effort into my outfit until she laughs and says, "Great costume. I love how you don't even care enough to wear a jersey or anything. Very cool." She smiles at me, exposing tiny white teeth completely unlike the sick yellow ones painted onto her cheek. She rubs her tiny gloved hands together while huddling up against me between the cool gusts of ocean wind. She turns her gruesome face up to mine and says, "Ah, it's so butt-fucking cold this time of year! We better start walking before it gets too late." And with that, she leaves my arm and starts to walk away. Numbly, I follow.

As the Earth's fiery mother star sinks beyond the hollow slabs of steel and stone, acting as a curtain against the slow, rolling ocean waves, the streets gradually start to fill with the pitter patter of werewolves, robots and slightly intoxicated loose women dressed poorly for the late October weather. While I enjoy this part of the holiday, I always find myself laughing at the expense taken to use the "dress like a movie prostitute for a night" pass that every girl gets once they turn the respectable age of eighteen. Don't get me wrong; if a girl fresh out of college wants to walk around in a sexy nurse or mouse (cat?) costume that consists of underwear and maybe a tiny hat or wire tail, that is completely within her right to do so. Halloween should forever be a day of complete aesthetic freedom for everyone; no person should be told what to wear or not to wear. With that said, maybe wearing a coat or a light sweater wouldn't have been a horrible idea for the poor group of women huddled together across the street. They screech and cluck at every gust of freezing wind that comes whipping at their exposed thighs and chests.

Harper and I exchange laughs about this as we start to get into the more populated part of the city with all the nightly themed bars and clubs. Weaving our way through the neon lit crowds of hooting drunk guys in crudely made Darth Vader costumes and flabby Magic Mike doppelgangers, we stay closer to the road to avoid the throngs of party goers lining the buildings eager to dance and drink.

As we are walking along the curb talking to each other about the correlations between G.G. Allen's baby dick and people who believe flat-earth theory, a guy dressed as Hulk Hogan (had he abused heroin and not steroids) crossing the sidewalk collides with Harper. The collision knocks Hogan to the ground while tossing Harper off the lip and onto the side of the road in front of a parked car.

"The fuck, bitch?! Watch your fuckin' step!" he yells at us in an angry redneck slur while adjusting the tassels on his costume. I hurry to pick Harper up off the ground to make sure she is okay. She shakily stands up, and for a second I am afraid she might be hurt. I am relieved a little once I see her smile up at me. She stands up, brushes the loose gravel off her mud stained blue jeans, and calmly says back, "Suck my ass, Hogan. And judging by the headband and sunglasses, I wouldn't doubt it was the first ass you've sucked tonight, either."

Hogan scoops up his shades from the curb before a fat Latino Bart Simpson could accidentally step on them and says, "That right, slut?" He puffs his chest out in a primal reflex after putting his fancy, bright red shades back on his even redder scowling face. As he balls his shaky hands, he approaches us in long swaying steps. His steel toe, snakeskin boots clicking and rawhide tassels swaying in a hypnotic zigzagging pattern across the sidewalk.

Using the curb as a four-inch boost, he tries to tower over us as he rants. "If you weren't already a corpse, I'd punch you in the suck hole then rape you dead. A stupid cunt like you deserves nothing less than the best, right Freddy Krueger?" He gestures to me with one fingerless, canary yellow leather glove. My patience with this asswipe is growing thin. I soon notice random people stopping to survey the scene. A loose half circle forms, slowly becoming a crude ring for a much-anticipated impromptu Wrestle-Mania show. Already I see people with their phones raised, waiting for a chance to get some of that sweet, copyright free YouTube cheddar.

As I am about to step in and end the conversation, Harper boldly says, "This is the reason why you'll die alone, Mr. Hogan. In a way I feel bad for you, but in a more humanitarian way, I'm glad that your rotten seed won't spread and further pollute the world with more thoughtless bullshit. You're alone tonight and will probably be alone every night for the rest of your miserable life. You want to know why? Well, big surprise, no one wants to be with an inbred cock sneeze who wears sunglasses at night." The surrounding crowd roars with laughter then slowly hushes. All attention is now on bizarro Hulk Hogan.

Hogan sways on the lip of the curb as he absorbs what has just been said to him. He then blurts out, "Say another fuckin' thing to me again, whore, and I'll kill you." He has time to raise one spindly arm out to Harper, as if to grab her, before I reach up to grab him by his bright red cutoff shirt with my left hand and slam his nose with a hard right. Not expecting my blow, he stumbles back down to the sidewalk and once again loses his shades in the crowd of spectators.

From outside of myself, I am amazed at how accurate my reflexes are. Apparently, all those years of karate and boxing lessons at the youth center were still very deeply ingrained in my brain. Every day after school from fifth to eleventh grade was spent enrolled in mixed martial arts or self-defense classes, always by my mom's force. I know she probably just wanted me to stay out of trouble while she was busy pulling a double shift at the hospital. You would think that after ten years of not having to use these skills that I would have pushed them out to make room for trivial things like *Seinfeld* dialogue or Stephen Lynch lyrics. My concern for Harper must have triggered this involuntary reflex and set in motion a tactical autopilot system of sorts. I can feel my muscles tightening and stance widening as I go into self-defense mode. Even through the bulky mask, my eyesight sharpens; I view everything in a vibrant, slow motion reel as I wait for his next move.

Hulk quickly scrambles to his feet. He squats into a runner's pose before letting out a guttural war cry that sounds like a dying moose, and then he boldly charges. Why he would warn me he was coming is beyond my comprehension. I brace myself as he lumbers forward.

With hot, rapid breaths fogging my face and eyes, I quickly whip off my mask and toss it to the ground by Harper's feet. The cool night air tickles at the tiny beads of perspiration on my nose and cheeks, and all at once I am aware of him gaining ground fast. Even with my delayed reaction, I see him coming from a mile away. I quickly side step to the right. Arms flailing, he dives headfirst into the parked car behind me. The car's alarm springs into life with horn blaring and lights flashing. Hogan seems to have impaled himself into the side door like a spray tanned harpoon until seconds later he falls limply to the curb, exposing a basketball sized dent in the side of some poor guy's minivan. The crowd goes wild. From all around me, I hear odd chanting and people yelling, "World Star! World Star!" over and over again while dozens of tiny cell phone cameras spotlight Hogan as he rolls around collecting gum and cigarette butts while clutching his undoubtedly sore head. Not wanting to fight this guy any more than I have to, I give him space to get up as I face him, waiting.

"Sucker punch me, you fuckin' pussy!" he screams through a red beard of blood flowing from his crushed nose. Thick drops of blood are dripping off his chin as he props himself up again. His teeth are gnashed together in an expression of pure hostility and embarrassment. Surely, the real Hulk Hogan would be very disappointed to be represented this way. I don't think this is lost on bizarro Hogan. He dramatically spits a bloody tooth into the gutter and makes a lazy attempt to wipe the drying blood off his face with his forearm, but he only smears it more. With his demented clown make-up, his eyes glow with morbid rage. I can feel his stubbornness to admit defeat and walk away like a man. I know now that if I don't knock this guy out, he will follow us around until I do, or he will maybe take out his aggression on someone else who can't defend himself (or herself) nearly as well. Once he picks himself up, he charges at me — his fists raised. As he shuffles forward, he screams, "After I beat your ass I'm gonna rape your..."

That beautifully crafted sentence is interrupted by a left hook and a right elbow to the throat that sends him folding to the curb twitching and choking. His veiny, pink eyes bulge out of his skull and his breaths become gurgled and short. I crouch down to ask him if he is done, and the look of immense pain and fear that I get back is enough to tell me yes. The rowdy crowd around me explodes in chanting and mocking laughter as I stand back up and dust myself off. From all sides, I have cardboard Ninja Turtles giving me sloppy high fives, Walter Whites fist bumping me, and various Deadpools of all shapes and sizes taking questionable selfies with the pulpy, disoriented mess that used to be the bronzed god of Worldwide Wrestling. I had half expected this and took the onslaught of loud admiration as patiently as I could, not wanting to have to repeat this whole testosterone fueled monkey match over again with some other tanked up idiot. I probably broke this guy's larynx without warrant, but I really don't think anyone would blame me for that after talking to him for more than five seconds. This may have been in the best interest of everyone. I step over the fetal remains of Mr. Hogan and approach Harper, who is still by the roadside where the altercation started.

"Are you okay, Harper?" I ask slightly out of breath, but still full of adrenaline. "He didn't hurt you, did he?" Her face is blank and even through the corpse paint, I can see the warm glow of her now rosy cheeks in the blinking neon and passing headlights.

"I'm fine," she finally says, still a thousand miles

away. "Let's get out of here before he gets up." She bends down and picks up my mask. Her hands tremble slightly as she passes it to me. I wipe the sweat out from the inside with my shirt before sliding it back on. She then grabs my hand and leads me through the crowd of gawking onlookers and noisy street traffic.

Once again, her demeanor has changed. Good job, dumbass. You managed to fuck up another perfectly avoidable situation. I probably embarrassed her, but I never would've hit that guy unless I thought we were in danger. I know I could have subdued him without breaking his nose, but that disrespectful shit coming out of his stupid pie hole was too much for me to tolerate. To be honest, I wanted to smash his face in when he called her a whore. As soon as he started threatening to kill her, I knew I had to take him down. I don't regret doing it even if it did make Harper upset. I firmly believe that some people deserve to swallow a few teeth now and again. We circled the block without any conversation and made our way back to her apartment building.

She stands outside her front door, facing me but looking down at her feet as if trying to think of something to say. Suddenly, she grabs my mask and tears it off of my face. With cold, grey hands, she pulls me down by the front of my hoodie and lands a plump, wet kiss firmly on my cold, slightly chapped lips. Our cold noses touch momentarily and, after little thought, both sets of lips graciously open and our tongues meet for the first time. The cold numbness of our lips slowly melts away against the frictionless heat steaming out of our mouths. All feeling leaves my body as I explore the inside of her mouth with my warm, slippery tongue as we talk and hum our silent language of lust.

The deep kiss ends mutually, and we stare at each other — stunned — for several moments. Harper says, "Thank you, Nick. That was the nicest thing anyone has ever done for me."

Being a dazed moron, I respond with, "Am I that good of a kisser?" She laughs, taking my floating hands in hers.

"No, Fart knocker. Beating up Hulk Hogan was one of the sexiest things I've ever seen in my life." She then lets go of my weightless hands and they drop limply to my sides. "I want to see you again next weekend. I'm a cheap date, so don't worry about renting a limousine or any fancy dinner reservations. Meet me here around eight on Saturday if you're interested. See you later, Nick. Thanks again for a great night." She steals another kiss before turning to walk inside, leaving me frozen on the moonlit curb.

A rigid statue misplaced in the city of freaks.

Chapter 13

A Condom in Reverse

A crisp, tender breeze carries along the scents and soul of autumn. Its mild coolness is not uncomfortable, but rather consoling. Almost warming. The fallen leaves are assorted in a mosaic on the ground. The ones still clinging to life somehow brighten the already radiant day, accenting the hues of oranges and reds as the sun sinks beneath the horizon. The clouds blush as the sun slips into the tree line. The waves softly serenade the world, coaxing it to succumb to the serenity of the moment. Carrying it to slumber.

One of the most glorious privileges of life in Maine is the fusion of coastal and forest terrains. The oaks and maples need not be sacrificed for the songs of the sea. The only sacrifices are that of commerce and recreation. That is a fair price for tranquility and sanctuary.

Nick sits with me, his arm resting on the bench behind me. In the chill, his warmth delicately kisses my neck and shoulders. The drifting clouds reflect off of his blue-grey eyes like falling rose petals. How long we have been sitting here together remains a mystery to me. I feel as if I could remain in this moment for eternity. There are no other bodies, no obligations, no uncertainties. There is only us.

Turning to face me, his prominent nose casts a slight shadow down his cheek as the sun says his final farewell. With the gentleness of the most skilled Yogi, Nick collects and then cradles my hands in his own. His eyes never leave my own. As the sun finally flickers out of existence, Nick says, "Harper, I need to ask you something."

The sounds of the waves begin to fade, as if manipulated by a volume knob.

Nick has my full attention.
I await his question.

The tempo of my heartbeat
overpowers all other
sound.
All other
thoughts.

Those blue eyes glance downward at our clasped hands for a moment.

They return to gaze into my own.

"Why did you kill him?"

In that moment, all sound and sensation ceased to exist. A harsh ringing quickly swells in the center of my head. The cold seizes my body, shackling me in place. The sky — once beautiful and warm — transforms before my eyes to putrid and raw. The oranges now green and infected. The falling rose petals now globs of decaying flesh.

Nick's lips begin to peel away from his mouth, the skin rolling upon itself like a condom in reverse. With torturous slowness, the skin continues to roll back, exposing the crimson, fleshy bone beneath. Bits of stringy, pink tissue resist the pull, but inevitably snap under the tension and then hang loosely from the sticky skull. As the skin peels further and further, the grotesque remnants of Nick's once handsome face dissolve like rotten sand. It slithers over his nose and beyond his eyes, leaving two grisly, sunken globes behind to stare back at me in disgust before dissolving out of existence.

The ringing screams around me, inside of me

and
        then...

Nothing.

Paralyzed.

My body is shaking like I'd spent the night in a walk-in refrigerator. My eyes adjust to the darkness. Straight ahead, my television begins to take shape. Cautiously, I tilt my head back and examine the wall just behind me. I've never been so excited to see a scrotum in my life. Instantly, I make the decision to never repaint that spot as long as I live in this place.

I'm in my apartment.
I'm okay.

How can a person who is such a huge, dripping wet pussy love the horror genre so much? I know that watching a scary movie or reading a horror novel before bed will make me hear all sorts of imaginary monsters in my apartment or will give me frighteningly realistic dreams when I'm finally able to fall asleep. But, I do it anyway. A year or so ago, I did some Internet research (I know, how reliable and valid!) and stumbled upon Aristotle's theory of catharsis. Or, something like that. He argued that people like all of this violent and scary shit as a means of purging all of the pent up *negative shit* we bury deep within ourselves. It's almost like a psychological enema. Psychologists these days claim that the opposite happens. Violence supposedly makes people more aggressive and watching or reading things like sappy erotica or humor help with the elimination of shit more (I guess I'm spot on when I say these genres are shit...). Buuuut, there's still the possibility that subjecting ourselves to the horror genre can help to reduce fear.

Well, I don't see my fear, or the skid marks in my under-drawers, reducing at all.

Refusing to leave the safety of my blanket pile just yet, I turn on the lamp that I keep beside my bed for **situations** like these. Light fills my room and my heart slows to a light jog. It's on its way to the mailbox rather than trying to catch the last bus home. I somehow find the courage to sit up and grab my cell phone from the windowsill:

1:00 AM.

The aftershock still makes it impossible for me to leave my "bed." It feels like the annoying sensation you get after using a weed whacker for hours, only dispersed throughout the entire body. For a moment, I think about texting Nick, but let's face it: most normal people are sound asleep by now, not having nightmares directed by David Cronenberg.

He would probably just laugh at you for being such a fuckin' pussy.

Accepting defeat, I grab the remote from beside my lamp and fill the emptiness with the sounds of Jewish comedy.

CHAPTER 14
YO' MAMA

It is Sunday morning.

As part of my weekend ritual, I take a little time out of my "busy" schedule to talk to my mom to see how she's doing. Still a full-time nurse in her fifties, she rarely lets a weekend go by without checking in with me. Any time I miss a Sunday call from my mother, it is usually because I pretend to be too busy. Ignoring the special Danzig ringtone that I tastefully picked out for her, I send a delayed text letting her know that I am "busy at work." It hardly seems worth it seeing as how she always leaves me an incredibly long, and guilt ridden, voicemail if I don't pick up the first time around.

Don't get me wrong. I love talking to her, but I hate the fact that I never have anything to say. She could go on and on about all the interesting things and people she encounters every day at the hospital, enough weird butt stories to fill an entire afternoon, and all I can ever say when she asks about my life is "not much." What do I tell my mom? Do I tell her that I moved to a progressive new city just to spend my days cleaning toilets and reading books? She stopped asking me about making new friends years ago, finally realizing that I probably never was going to come out of my hard antisocial shell.

I decided to call her today since I actually have something to talk about. I'll admit, I was initially hesitant to tell my mom about Harper, but after all that's happened, I think I could use some advice. I took this moment in between her telling me a story about a guy who came in last week after attempting to eat a bottle of wood glue, apparently trying to make the next viral YouTube video, and laid it all down.

"So... I think I met a girl..." I say rather shyly. I wait for the inevitable.

I hear the quick whooshing sound of her lungs filling from six hundred miles away, and then her voice explodes. "OH MY GOSH, NICK! Are you serious?! When do I get to meet her?! What's her name?! Is she pretty?! Are you two love birds engaged yet?!"

"Alright Mom, calm down. We aren't even really dating at this point. We have hung out a couple times, but nothing too serious. And yes, she is very pretty."

She squeals in jubilation at the news and then says, "Oh, Nick, I am so happy for you! Well, what's her name? Don't keep me in suspense, hunny."

"Her name is Harper. We met a little while ago through my job at the cleaners. We clicked almost immediately as friends, but things are really starting to get... serious. It's crazy, Mom, but I think this girl really likes me. I have never felt this way about any girl in my life."

"Except your mother. Of course," she jokingly tacks onto the end.

I make exaggerated gagging noises back at her and then say, "Ew, Mom, who do you think I am? Sigmund Freud?

"You know what I mean, dipshit," she says with a tinge of that slightly sassy, no-nonsense tone that I heard all too often as a kid.

"Mom," I start to say before hesitating slightly to gather my thoughts, "I don't know how to ask you this, but..."

"It's about your diphallia, isn't it?" she says bluntly, wanting to get right down to the bone of the matter. "You want to know how to confront Harper with the facts. Or does she know already?"

"Of course she doesn't know!" I say, feeling more embarrassed than angry at my mom's bluntness. "If she did, we wouldn't be having this conversation."

"Calm down, hun, I just want to help." Abandoning her Dr. Phil persona, "Are you afraid she might not approve of your... um..."

"Well, yeah, I have no idea how she will react, but I know she probably won't be that open-minded."

My mom sighs deeply and then says, "You are too quick to assume, hunny. This girl must be special to you if you are considering telling her."

"I didn't say that! I just know that eventually things will end up..."

"Nick," she interrupts me, "I know you have been dealt a bad hand, but you can't let it rule your life. There is no possible way you can predict the outcome to every situation you will ever have. Life is about making mistakes and learning from them, and you will get rejected along the way. And the rejection never stops, Nick. Not when you're thirty, forty, or eighty. You can either look at life through one lens, the one where every day is a pointless challenge and nothing is gained, only lost, or you can look at it through the lens of hopeful understanding. Only when you frame the two together can you truly start to see life for what it is. You see, hun, without the constant obstacles we face with every moment of every breath, the best things in life would barely be worth anything. It's the suffering and tribulations that make love and happiness so great, not the bliss itself. It is the journey to finding love that makes it so fulfilling, to know nothing else would rob love of all its magical qualities. What good is a magician if you know how all his tricks are done, right?"

I am in shock of what I just heard. You would think I climbed into some archaic phone booth and called Plato like so many bad Bill and Ted movies. I am no closer to finding an answer.

"I guess... listen, let's change the subject. Got any good butt stories from last—"

"Look, if Harper feels the same way about you as

you do about her, then she will be accepting of who you are. She will love you for your mind, not your body. And if she does have a problem, oh well. She isn't good enough to be dating my son, then."

I chuckle a little then say, "Yeah, because I am such a catch."

"Seriously, hun," that no-nonsense tone edging in her voice, "you need to accept the unchangeable. Your condition is no reason to hate on yourself. I worry about you, Nick. Being alone all the time can't be good for anyone. Look what it did to that poor Ted Kaczynski."

I try to keep a less defensive tone and say, "I'm not alone, Mom. I told you, I have Harper now."

"Yes... now. But you can't avoid telling her forever."

I went silent. There was nothing I could say. She was completely right. Yes, I had Harper now, but it was under false pretenses. I think I love her, yet, I haven't let her get to know me well enough to actually see the whole picture. I wanted an answer, and God dammit, that's what I got. Not exactly what I wanted to hear, but that is often the nature of truth. Unpleasant to hear, but solid in practice.

"Thanks, Mom," I finally say after she leaves me room to think. "Listen, I gotta go get a head start on my laundry. Same time next Sunday?"

"You know it, dumplin. And please, Nick, remember what I said. Love you."

"I love you too, Mom."

With that, we hang up. Sitting in my apartment

now, vaguely listening to the mice scratch and chirp behind the walls, I wonder if I even have what it takes to man-up and tell Harper the truth.

Chapter 15
The Divine Patchwork

Gently, I do my best to draw on my liquid eyeliner without looking like a ghoul or a victim of domestic abuse. I'll never be able to fathom how so many women are able to draw those tidy little cat's eye swooshes on their eyelids. My results always end up looking like I hired Michael J. Fox as my evening make-up artist. Maybe this is one of the reasons why I never truly dated... but, I'm sure the fact that I make a fart joke every ten minutes has more to do with my lack of a love life than me being too lazy to use fancy make-up techniques.

*Don't you think you were a little, erm, forceful about this whole date thing? You sort of put the dude on the spot, didn't you? Of course he wasn't going to say no; he's **a nice guy**.*

Yeah, Nick is **a nice guy**. Which is why I had to be the one to make the first move. I couldn't just wait around while he grew the balls to ask me out. The guy had tried to insist on going to some fancy-pants place across town, but if I can't pronounce the name of the place, I definitely can't afford to eat there. And I'll be damned if I'll let **a nice guy** pay $40 for something that looks like I wiped it out of my ass crack after a bad case of the Hershey Squirts. To quote Miss Megan, **Dating Extraordinaire**, *"Some of the nicer ones are a little shy, too."*

*Mmm, kay. BUT, let's say he is **a nice guy** who has no interest in you. Would he politely decline or accept out of pity, or even necessity? If he were to decline, that would make work crazy awkward, and he might have been worried about hurting any feelings that hide beneath that calloused exterior. You basically gave him no choice but to say yes.*

I pull my flat iron through my hair. This is the first time it's seen any action for about a year (*still more attention than your vag has gotten...*), and I'm trying my best not to sizzle my neck in the process. What a wonderful accessory a nice, juicy burn-blister would make for a first date. It's not the type of hickey I was hoping to be branded by tonight. I watch as my already straight hair becomes bereaved of any texture. The warmth left by the iron radiates through my sweater— teal, not black for a change — which I'm thankful for, considering my landlord is too cheap to include heat in the rent, and my broke ass can't invest in that sort of luxury. Hey, at least this forced monk-level of poverty is forcing me to enjoy the smaller things in life.

I stare back at my reflection. Scrutinizing. Second-guessing my choice of clothing.

If the heat is cranked up at the eatery, them pits are goin' be sweating…

Whatever. I don't care.

…dude. Seriously?

Fuck, I sort of do care.

Holy shit, is *this* what girls go through before every date? This is exhausting. I wonder if guys are subjected to this amount of emotional and mental torment before finally meeting up for a romantic rendezvous with that "someone special." Do they tediously trim each individual hair on their faces? Do they hyper-analyze their clothing choices as if they're the words in a Hemingway novel?

I find myself sifting through my memories as I unplug the hair iron from the cracked power outlet (for the love of Gandhi, don't let me electrocute myself today; all of the hair straightening would've been for nothing). Honestly, I can't remember ever going through this type of pre-date prep work. The last time I can even remotely recall being close to this lovesick was when I was sixteen. He was a quiet, Middle Eastern-looking dude named Jason Jadallah. His floppy afro and swarthiness had me completely enamored. I don't know what it is about those ethnic guys, Arabs, Mediterraneans, Italians, Israeli-Jews, but fuck me sideways, do they get me going. Come to find out, Juicy-Jadallah had a love of cocaine and Jezebelian women. Maybe this preference was a way of paying tribute to the Israel-Jordan Peace Treatise. Anyway, it left me heartbroken and assigned me to my traditional role of just another bro.

In my pathetic case, bros never came before hoes...
Too bad. So sad.

Impatiently, I wrap the still hot flat iron quickly and set it on the yellowing bathroom sink. A pair of heels creates a hollow rhythm above me as they make their way across the apartment upstairs. They probably belong to a classy new suitor decked-out in ill-fitting clothing and two types of Hepatitis (gotta' catch em all). I've still yet to see the dude living above me. He brings more broads home in a week than the amount of men I've been with in my life-time.
Have I ever been on a true, honest-to-God date?
My bottom lip instinctively hides between my teeth (*good thing you decided against lipstick, ey?*) as I dig deeper, rifling through my teen years. School dances weren't my thing: the model first date for most preteens. Not one boy ever asked me to a school dance. Maybe it was due to my public loathing of school functions or possibly the fear that my dancing would put Jim Carey to shame. The times I went anywhere with a male were to spend time as friends. I was the *Slapstick Sidekick* — never the

Sexy Sweetheart.

What about all of the time you spent with Will? The two of you made public appearances as a couple. That has to count for something.

I glance back up at the mirror, making eye contact with my carefully outlined green orbs of repentance. Despite the amount of time Will and I had spent together, there was never a time I went out of my way to get gussied up for an outing.

Not. One. Time.

It isn't that I didn't care about Will. Seriously, I did care for him and I'll always love him in a way. The type of love we shared was more of the type of love shared among the best of friends rather than the romantic love girls read about in unrealistic books with overly symbolic titles or the type of love people write shitty ballads about. Will was a great person. He put up with my shit and never made me feel alienated. But, there was always the feeling that something was missing. We went through all of the motions necessary to have a "relationship," but it'd never felt like we were truly "together." I often find myself wondering whether this had to do with his struggles with mental health, or if my lack of affection is what shoved the spacer between us. Was I incapable of that feeling Barry White and Prince sang about for so many years?

Then, I met Nick.

No other boy, man — or woman, for that matter — has made my heart do a hop, skip, and flamboyant jump the way Nick does. The way his soft curls delicately frame his well-defined face, how the blue hue of his eyes accents his not-quite-olive-not-quite-bronze skin. His nose prominent but not grotesque in size. He's like some divine patchwork of all of the most beautiful features of every European and Middle Eastern ethnicity blended in the most alluring of ways. Truly, he is God's gift to women.

How is it possible that such an exquisite human-being doesn't have a girlfriend? Even more so, how does a man oozing with so much sex appeal have *bad* luck with the ladies, as he claims? This could've been a flat out lie, but there was a sad sincerity in his eyes that makes me wonder if there's more to Nick than meets the eye (although, what my eyes do behold is evidence of a supreme creator; I might even pick up a Bible soon). The avoidance of the topic of relationships and his lack of social media accounts are both red flags that there's something from his past that he has carefully tucked away like an embarrassing fetish porno at the bottom of a sock drawer.

Stop over-analyzing; Nick isn't some T.S. Eliot poem. He accepted your invitation, so roll with it. Besides, you would never have a chance with a dude this hot unless he was damaged in some way. Even if there was some sort of shit-storm that wiped out the majority of humanity, leaving you as the only female to have relations with (emotional or otherwise), a guy that hot would choose loneliness and the company of his hands. Maybe whatev-

er he is hiding is a blessing in disguise. Do you seri-ously think a dude of model-level attractiveness would consider even speaking to you if he were perfect in every conceivable way? Get the fuck out of here. Enjoy him while you can, and maybe someday he will open up to you about his issue(s), whatever it/they may be.

Well, we all have our secrets.
And some of us have our regrets.

The three sharp knocks on the door make me jump forward, and I almost knock my face against the low-hanging light above the bathroom mirror. That'd be just my luck to bash my idiot face off a hot light bulb. An open wound is a lovely facial accent for a first date. The red would *really* give the green of my eyes an extra pop.
I collect my thoughts, give myself one last survey in the mirror, and flip off the light.

It's show time.

CHAPTER 16
THE PEPPERMINT PANDA

"Hey guys, welcome to *Le Nain Chic*. My name is Chelsea. Table for two?" the short, bubbly blonde girl who couldn't be a day over eighteen pleasantly asks as Harper and I approach the large, black silk draped, gold rimmed podium at the mouth of the restaurant. I regard the fancy decor with some good luck on my part, having blown the chance to get a table at an oddly similar French restaurant across town that I stupidly let Harper turn down out of common courtesy. The gold tasseled drapes around the waiting area walls were tastefully hung to disguise the drab post office like feel of the tiny waiting area that was now starting to fill with other ill-prepared couples. Beyond the big wooden podium, I could see some people eating and talking at private tables, black silk tablecloths neatly folded around the dull, rounded edges of each one. The clear crystal tumblers containing several pearl white roses at every table momentarily convinces me that we narrowly got into a relatively fancy place at the last minute. Any chance I have of making it out of this date in one-piece hinges solely on the level of customer satisfaction received from a place whose name, I later Googled, means "The Fancy Midget" in French. With no way of knowing or being able to back out now, I forge on.

"Yes, please," I say with a whiney, girlish pitch in my voice that is way too loud over the clinking and clattering of patrons eating and pots banging somewhere unseen beyond the partially walled waiting area. I dryly clear my throat, apologizing to no one in particular, and sheepishly follow Harper and the bouncy blonde Chelsea to our table towards the back wall. My palms are greased with sweat and my chest cavity feels far too big for my skin. I mentally coach myself as we weave our way past other hungry couples to our lonely table in the back corner. Once we get there, slide out our chairs, and sit down, Chelsea hands us two poorly laminated, comically oversized menus. "Take a moment to browse the menus, and a server will be with you guys shortly — and please don't forget to try an order of our lemon spritzer club sauce that goes great with our chicken parfaits or shrimp scampi platter options." Flashing a glossy, post-cheerleader smile and a slight nod, she strolls back to her blocky Trojan Horse post to seat the next arriving couple.

Having no appetite whatsoever, I pretend to browse the menu while I look around at the endless array of miscellaneous garbage that is strung up on the over lacquered, lunch bag brown, wood paneled walls. The room we currently sat in had none of the sophistication or class of the walled in waiting area. It was as if Chelsea had led us through a dimensional rip and seated us in an entirely different restaurant on an alternate timeline where *Le Nain Chic* is actually *Slappy Sue's Family Feedbag Emporium*. The inside interior is littered with vintage bicycles, cheaply produced movie posters from the forties, and various mounted moose and deer heads with obnoxiously colored, dust filmed fedoras hanging off each dull, graying antler. Everywhere I look I am forced to take in some forgotten relic of the last century that was presumably lost for a reason. It would be easy to confuse the dining room in this place for a publicly funded museum or low rate pawnshop if everyone wasn't sitting around noisily eating frozen cube steak disguised as gourmet sirloin.

I start to wonder why Harper picked this place for our first date. I assume that it was probably due to it being a convenient two blocks from her apartment. I had offered meeting her outside of her apartment to drive us across town to another (hopefully classier) fancy French restaurant, even secretly making reservations a couple days ahead of time in case she said yes, but she insisted she didn't want to waste my gas when she heard of a decent spot just down the street.

Glancing at her over the huge manifold spread menus, my nerves quake and shudder like an old wet dog left outside in a cold April rainstorm. Her shiny crimson hair is sleek and draped behind her, allowing her bare shoulders to show over the incredibly sexy, strapless dress she is wearing now that she has removed her sweater. Her eyeliner and blush are faint, only there to accentuate her already stunning facial features. I steal quick glimpses of her now and again when she isn't looking, unable to take my mind off of how flawlessly beautiful she is no matter the setting.

I try to force myself to read the unusually long and noisy menu propped up in front of me. The words blur and swim together, forming a kaleidoscope of text as I feel my eyes desperately pulling to focus and adjust to the whirlpool of appetizers and side options. I can't even remember the last time I went on a date, let alone with someone I felt so deeply for. I had to do this right, or I would end up back where I started.

Alone.

Needing badly to take an anxious piss, I playfully slap the menu onto the tabletop and casually say, "Be right back. I'm going to go wash my hands." I push my chair out and clumsily walk towards the huge flamboyant sign shaped like a giant, cornflower blue tampon. It spun slowly, creating the words "Restrooms" in honey butter yellow letters across its slick, tubular surface with each passing turn. I near its hypnotic spinning as I race my way through the maze of talking animatronic moose heads and randomly placed flat screen TV's all simultaneously playing grainy reruns of Happy Days on full blast.

As I hurriedly wobble my way to the bathroom with a bladder full of what feels like rancid Tabasco sauce, I graze past other couples eating and enjoying themselves over cheap, but aesthetically pleasing, scentless candles and overpriced cocktails with tiny wooden umbrellas lined with flimsy, floral tissue paper draped delicately over the large granular salted rims. I couldn't help but feel petty and cynical about this whole thing, feeling like this entire situation was completely pointless and surely doomed from the start. Even if we hadn't bravely picked "The Classy Midget" as our exclusive dining experience for the night, I am sure that I would have managed to inadvertently fudge things up somehow. It has always been doomed, really, because Logic predetermined the outcome for me, but I force the idea aside, determined to stay positive. Fuck you, Logic. This time Double or Nothing Nick is going for broke.

I pump myself up with pleasant, all highly unlikely, hypothetical outcomes to tonight's date as I slip past the cacophony of banging cupboards and harsh authoritative shouting slipping out between the loosely swinging kitchen doors to my left and enter the men's bathroom. There are two urinals, two sinks, and three psychiatric ward green stalls to match the rest of the splotchy, moisture rotted walls crammed into the tiny, dark space that serves as part of my "luxurious dining experience." It took much mental straining to fight back all the shitty comments and unnecessary critiques constantly blooming up in my spiteful, narrow mind as I tread cautiously, always mindful of random shallow puddles of sticky urine, across the faux marble tiling. I approach the closest urinal and find the porcelain rim to be sprinkled with hazel and blonde pubic hairs of various lengths and textures, reminding me vaguely of the colorful mixed drinks being served just outside the door. Sickened, I hurriedly unleash the boys. As I am expelling the sick, stingy liquid from my waxy, overanxious kidneys, a voice comes drifting out from behind one of the closed stall doors to my right.

"Sup man!? What's crackin?"

I stop mid-stream(s) and quickly glance back over my right shoulder toward the racially ambiguous, echoey voice, not sure what to say. I see a pair of legs under the gap of the middle stall door and realize that I am not alone. As a clumsy, mediocre response comes to me after several awkward seconds tick by, the unseen man says, "Oh, not much, just on break right now. Hey, man, listen. You know that chick that we met at the ULTRA Club last weekend? Yeah, the one in the slutty zebra print cocktail dress with the no panties that kept ball gazing me from across the bar. Welp, guess who porked her in the Sizzler's parking lot, Cuz?!"

By this time, I realize that it was some uber-cool guy, most likely college educated, talking on his cell phone while taking a dump. Disgusted, I shake then re-holster the double barrel and am about to flush the urinal with my elbow when I overhear more.

"That's right!"

"What? Nah, man, it ain't like that. I mean... yeah, I got a rash and shit, but it don't mean that bitch gave me the herp or nothin.

"I don't care what Frankie told you! You know he's just jealous of my swagger ever since that night I showed him up on...what?

There are a few moments of tense silence before the voice explodes out in a fit of rage.

"Then why the fuck didn't you tell me then! That toad lookin' motherfucker got the herp from that zebra slut, and you didn't think to give me the courtesy of a heads up?! So fuckin' weak, man. What? Yeah, it showed up a day or two after we scrogged, what of it?

"You know... so what?! Big fuckin deal, bro. I get a rash once in a while! It's not like I have AIDs or motherfuckin' syphilis or something. It's that filthy, no panty wearin' knob-goblin's fault anyway that I even got this shit. You wait until I see Frankie's big stupid face again...he...oh, come on! Don't trip on me like that, man.

"Whateva nigga, listen, I be calling to see if you could hook a homie up with Michelle's number. No, man, I just need to talk to her is all... nothing more.

"Yeah... yeah, alright. I'll give you a call when I get out of here. Peace."

Realizing that I have overstayed my right to eavesdrop, I flush the urinal and quickly go to a sink before hearing the mystery caller's toilet flush a short time after I turn on the rusty faucet. I am rushing to wash my hands and get out of there when I hear one of the peeling stall doors behind me slam open, rattling on its splotchy, paint bubbled hinges. Startled, I look up in the mirror placed directly above the sink just in time to see a man in a red vest and black, ironed slacks come sauntering out of the only occupied stall. His low, angular brow causes a deep shadow to form across his flat, stony face as he steps out under the one naked sixty-watt bulb dangling just above our heads. Tall and lean, his strong shoulders and slumped posture tell me that while he probably frequented the gym, mostly lifting free weights, booze mixed with poor eating habits and lack of cardio were slowly eating away at the youthful figure that he so vainly squandered. His stained vest lay open to expose a forming potbelly that pushed stubbornly at the ashy grey button up shirt underneath his crayon red vest.

We lock eyes for a moment in the dirty, graffiti scratched reflection of the mirror before he coldly turns and walks out the door and back into the twanging, mumbling atmosphere of the restaurant without attempting to use the sink next to me to wash his hands. I linger a bit longer at the towel dispenser just to make sure that I don't run into him out in the dining area, and then I slowly make my way back to the table.

"Jesus, Nick, did you bust a nut or something? You were gone a while," Harper jokes naggingly at me as I pull out my seat and sit down across from her.

"Nah, it's crazy though. I was in there and a guy on his phone was..."

Just before I could finish my thought, the waiter slides up to the side of the table, and we both turn to acknowledge him. With his little red vest, slick black slacks, and tiny notepad with detachable pen in hand, he introduces himself as Henry and asks what we would like to drink.

I freeze in terror at the sudden realization that the guy in the bathroom is our waiter. His cold, vacant eyes scan mine for any inkling of judgment, knowing I had heard all about his itchy night at Sizzler's. I insist that Harper order first so I can desperately rake my mind for an escape route out of this. There is no way I can possibly eat anything that this sexual deviant was in the natural vicinity of. From where I am sitting, I can almost see the parasitic bodies dragging and gnawing away at his cheesy, porous skin, burrowing ever deeper into stringy folds of dying muscle covering his soon to be brittle bones. His newly infected sores fading and reappearing across his thin, cracked lips and slender, stubble-lined cheeks. Oozing thick, yellow liquid so vile that the putrid, acidic smell was beginning to waft over to me from across the table.

"Sir? Have you decided on what you would like to

drink, or do you need more time?"

I hazily snap back out of the sycophantic day-dream and calmly say, "Sorry, I will need a little more time. Thanks."

Obviously annoyed at my inability to order a drink for myself, he throws me a cringey smirk and hurries off towards the kitchen.

"You okay, Nick?" Harper asks once Henry Herpes-A-Lot is out of earshot. "You've been acting weird ever since you got back from the bathroom. Is something wrong?"

"I... suddenly don't feel so great. Do you mind if I step outside for a little bit?"

She regards me from across the table with some suspicion. She then worriedly says, "Yeah, I didn't think this place was gonna be that great, either. To tell you the truth, this is my first time here, and I'm not so sure it was such a great idea. Is it too late to go somewhere else?" Her dark rimmed eyes plead with me not to be upset with the unintentionally poor choice she has made, and I weaken at the sight of her wide, hopeful expression.

"Of course not. The night is young," I say, feeling much better knowing that I wouldn't have to explain why I couldn't order food from a guy too dumb to wear a prophylactic while fucking a complete stranger in the parking lot of a subpar family-style restaurant chain. Before Henry has time to come back and inadvertently infect us with his crotch craters, Harper and I grab our coats from the back of our chairs and slip out the front exit back into the stale, frozen November night.

"Sorry again about that. Something felt off about that place once we got in there. I'm sure we can find another spot to grab food at that isn't decorated like an old couple's garage sale," Harper says over her shoulder in a semi-playful tone as we walk out of the spotlighted lobby and down the dark, orange-lit road. We walk aimlessly towards the busier business district of the city where trendy boutiques and coffee shops line the solemn, weightless streets. Her crimson hair bobs and wavers in the shifting night air as our echoing footsteps bounce off the nearby walls and windows of the towering concrete boxes that border and confine us at every turn.

Walking close in tow, I mumble back that it was fine and continued to curse myself for having the worst dating game known to man. Only I could end up taking a girl on a date and then leave before we even get to eat because of an insane fear of contracting a case of the sack nasties from Henry, the soon to be Valtrex recipient.

I will admit, though, I take slight comfort in knowing that no matter what my attitude is about this date that the outcome is completely out of my hands. That dreaded weight on my chest to perform at my best is dissipating, and I can actually feel myself physically straightening back up; imitating more freely the walk and movements of a real man.

Touché, Logic. Touché.

I marvel at the all-knowing, clairvoyant powers of Logic while at the same time feeling like a slave to it. My stride is broken when Harper stops short and says, "Hey, this place looks fun," indicating the guarded doors surrounded by flashing, swirling lights just off to my left. I crane my neck up to the huge, luminescent sign casting a rainbow of shadows down onto the sidewalk at my feet, floating and seething majestically just above the thick, black, leather buttoned doors.

The *Peppermint Panda*, it reads. The two large P's act as naughty electric pinwheel nipples for the huge mural of a shaggy black and white panda climbing a bamboo stripper pole placed just behind the sign.

"Ugh... I think that's a strip club," I say — confused — to Harper as she walks towards the doors and is stopped by one of the huge black tie social meat mountains hired to do security.

As she is pulling out her I.D. for them to inspect, she turns to me and says, "Yeah, should be a better time than that T.G.I. Fridays abortion that we just avoided. Are you coming in or not?" She steps aside to let other people in line pass through while waiting for me to respond. The idea of going anywhere even remotely sexual was not on my agenda, but I couldn't just let the love of my life walk into a seedy strip club without feeling somewhat responsible for what would happen to her once she crossed the threshold and naively delved into the grimy, pink underbelly of the live nude circuit. I had always been too awkward, not to mention sexually ignorant, to muster up enough courage to go to a strip club on my own. I know I only have one choice. Grudgingly, I take one last look back before fishing out my I.D. and stepping cautiously through the heavy swinging doors to that waiting foreign space with Harper, hand in hand.

Once inside, I am taken aback by how much different the decor and atmosphere are opposed to the run down jizz shack that I had pictured in my head. Aside from the elevated platforms and long fireman poles that are required to efficiently run a club such as this, the chromed-out tables and comfily padded leather booths look as if they came from an upscale dining suite or Las Vegas lounge. Vibrant, velvet drapings over the harsher necessities and utilities, such as the sound system and buffet carts, give the place a soft yet playful feel that isn't lost on my semi-innocent sensibilities. The scene I had envisioned for all strip clubs everywhere was fairly basic: a dirty room full of skeezy, down on their luck men drooling and sweating over scabby, C-section scarred women with lackluster expressions plastered on their tired, strung out faces as they flap their veiny sweater puppets to an endless loop of Bon Jovi hits while grease stained hands shove and prod crumbly dollar bills into any available orifice. Had I known that my drab and highly ignorant assumption was false, I surely would have been a regular customer at many local strip joints during those lonely, mundane years of my early twenties.

Taken by complete surprise, the first few dancers

I see as we walk towards an available booth off by the bar are phenomenally attractive. With tight, flexible bodies and legs that went on forever, I wonder briefly what brought something so inherently beautiful and physically flawless to a career of stripping. I know the answer is surely student loans, but the idea of these beautiful women spending their nights entertaining common, run of the mill, carbon-based life forms such as myself is perplexing. To think, only a couple hundred years ago these women would have been considered sexual goddesses, worthy of only the highest caliber of virile men in hopes of somehow capturing that special, hypnotizing glow that emanates only around the ones who are truly born in God's striking image. I know strippers make a killing in tips and whatnot, but I still view it as beneath them morally and intellectually; as genetically superior beings, society as a whole should treat them as such.

I could see a few girls on stage now swaying and kicking around the poles as we sat down in our cozy, horseshoe-shaped booth and eye each other briefly over the pounding subwoofer hanging just six feet over our heads.

A tiny, silk-skinned black girl with the widest hips I have ever seen in my life approaches our table. Her perky B-cup breasts are dewy with spray on glitter, and at first I fight the urge to stare at them as they bounce deliciously up to our table. She leans deeply across the table and sets down two napkins in front of us. Her dark chocolate nipples slide across its cool surface, leaving behind two faint double rainbows that even Bob Ross would surely have been proud of. Her tiny, slightly chafed voice strains to project over the air bending bass and driving repetitive beats that flood the room.

"Hey guys! My name is Jade. Can I get you two started with some drinks?" She hands us a menu that is a quarter of the size of the one given to us at *The Classy Midget*. She waits patiently, stiletto heels clicking and breasts lightly bopping to the song currently pumping out onto the room, while we both scan through the assorted drinks. Once again, my menu dyslexia kicks in, and all I can see is alphabet soup where drink orders should be. I turn to Harper and tell her to surprise me with first drink picks, and she all too eagerly agrees.

"We'll have two Mexican Tract Infections, please!" Harper finally yells to Jade. After quickly jotting it down in her tiny notebook that she keeps only God knows where, Jade graciously turns and clicks toward the bar. Watching her leave, I admire the thick, creamy texture of her impossibly well-rounded, chocolate-dipped ass and note that her lemon yellow, rhinestone thong is only further accentuating this point. Surely, she will be burning a big yellow Y into the impressionable foreground of my mind for days to come.

While we wait for our drinks, Harper and I watch the various dancers currently on stage performing for a small group of men that had congregated towards the front of the room. Resembling more of a gymnastics tournament than your typical peep show routine, these girls effortlessly defied gravity with intricate leg work and endless upper body strength all while managing to tease the crowd with meticulously timed splits and jaw dropping choreographed twerking. When our drinks come a short time later, I am already too entranced by the show to react to Harper grabbing my hand and pulling me towards the front with the other spectators. I fight it at first, gesturing to my drink like it is fixed to the table and couldn't be moved. With those seductive green eyes fixed to mine and the touch of her soft fingertips on my arm, my opposition crumbles apart like expired powdered donuts. I grab my Tract Infection and follow Harper across the blanketed space of lasers and flashing lights to the front.

***

The next five hours went by in a frenzy of loose cash and sour drinks. Once the liquor hit me, all my inhibitions and shame melted away in a sea of foamy orange fizzy water and dissonant, flashing lights. I was left with nothing inside but the fully untethered joy of a guy truly living for the first time. The constant worry and speculation that relentlessly eats needlelike holes through my feeble psyche were all but gone as I drank and laughed my way into oblivion. Dancing and tossing money without worry was something that felt unnatural, but spiritually invigorating to me, much like scuba diving or skydiving is for some people. Only now do I completely understand why it is considered a common rite of passage to most men.

After ordering countless more drinks and requesting the same Future song three times in a row (which they willingly played), Harper finally reached a point where she too was feeling the spiritual uplift of the mood-altering substances that were surging through us — poisoning and hardening our livers. As the night progressed, a loose pile of money had collected at the foot of the main stage, and when Future came on for a fourth and final time, Harper proceeded to grab wads of cash out of the pile and fart them at the unsuspecting strippers currently performing. Now, when I say, "fart them at the strippers," I mean that she would take a fistful of bills and simply make sloppy fart noises as she hucked fat, sweaty wads at them while they danced on and off stage. Eventually, Capri and Unique stopped twerking long enough on the bill littered stage to see this. Finding little to no humor in someone playing with their hard-earned cash, they got the meat mountains to come and not so gently escort us outside after insisting we pay our bill.

Completely sloshed, we stagger and sway back up the road, all the time laughing and hooting like howler monkeys newly escaped from the zoo. With complete drunken anonymity to the bitter night air, the trip seemed all too short as we got to the big, empty apartment front.

"Alright, great date, buddy," I say nonsensically without much regard to its meaning. "I gotta call a cab so I don't end up in the drunk tank tonight." With too much effort, I get my paper-thin phone out of my front pocket and blindly scroll the directory for a cab. As I'm scrolling through the fogged-out pane of my pocket computer for the fifth time with stupid, regressed fingers unable to work the simplest of mechanisms, the phone is slapped out of my hand, and Harper is pulling me into her warm essence — embracing me with soft, supple lips that call out for mine. Deja' vu hits me hard, and suddenly I am shoved back to that time not so long ago when I thought I would never experience this feeling of cosmic oneness ever again. The moment lasts forever until it ends all too soon, and she breathes these words to me in a puff of rolling steam. The words seem to linger in the frozen, black air that fills the vacant space between our still hungry lips.

"You could stay here tonight."

This isn't good. If she wants what I think she does, then I will have to sober up quick and do some explaining. On the other hand, I can't expect her to let me string her along forever. What the fuck am I expecting to get out of all this by telling lies and avoiding her, anyway? I know prolonging this charade is only worsening the situation, but I honestly don't know what else to do. There is a one in a million chance that she is into guys with split pikes, and even if she is, I don't know if I would be okay with that. I look at myself in such a negative way that I can't truly appreciate all the good things in my life. It wouldn't be fair for me to drag Harper down into the pits of cynicism with me. At the same time, it seems as if she has already made that descent on her own. Still, I know I am powerless from stopping the one huge flaw I have from constantly holding me back.

The only two choices I have are to either spend the night at her apartment or dig my phone out of the leaf filled gutter and call a cab.

I belch out the first answer that comes to my mind.

"Ahhm... sure."

Chapter 17

Mad About Jew

"Welcome to my humble abode, Nicholas. Take off your shoes, or keep them on — whatever gets you going — and make yourself at home. There isn't much to drink in the fridge, but the city water flows like wine." My speech isn't slurred, so I can't be *completely* shitfaced. Unless I'm so drunk that what sounds like sophisticated diction is actually more like post root canal ramblings.

A week ago, I'd been questioning whether my budget could handle buying a full-size mattress to replace the pathetic, heaping pile of blankets on the floor. I'm internally fist-pumping in triumph that I'd decided to spend the cash. Yeah, I'd only been able to afford the mattress, no box spring, but it's still a *real* bed. How awkward would it be to bring a guy to your apartment only to show him your dog bed on the floor? Yup, this is where I sleep. Right next to my water dish...

Even with the alcohol in full effect, my heart anxiously drums inside of my chest. This is the first time anyone has come into my apartment, and this is the first time I've ever invited a guy I had romantic intentions for into my place. I hope my forwardness doesn't come off as slutty, but Nick *is* plastered and is in no condition to drive home. For being hammered, he's still as handsome as fuck. There isn't even a hint of a drunken blush on his cheeks (maybe that sexy olive-bronze tint of his serves as camouflaging), but his giddiness and confident swagger say otherwise. Nick is not a swaggerer and usually has a reserved self-consciousness about him. Seeing him so comfortable with himself makes my heart happy.

The corners of his eyes gently crinkle as he smiles (fuck, he is going to age well). "Water is probably all I should be drinking at this point, anyway. South Harbor's water is full of minerals and chlorine, just the way I likes it." Carefully, he pulls his thick sweatshirt up and off himself. I see this happen in slow motion like I'm in an even lower-budget version of *Magic Mike* where the guys don't shave their chest hair. I catch a glorious glimpse of the happy trail bearding his belly button and almost — almost — need a change of panties. His voice isn't mushy at all. Actually, it has more fluidity to it, like the alcohol had removed the filter most moderately intelligent human-beings possess. You'd expect a person as sloshed as Nick has to be to sound a lot like a junked-out frat boy. This isn't the case. Somehow, he's a classy(ish) drunk.

Nick realizes that there's no furniture in my apartment after a few slow visual sweeps. He carefully leans against the kitchen counter that serves as a sort-of divider between the kitchen and the living room/bedroom. The angle of his casual counter seating (leaning) causes the buttons of his light blue plaid shirt (odd choice for Nick, but I guess he was trying to gussy himself up for our outing) to almost give under the tension created. Internally, I'm using all of my brainpower to telekinetically tug at these buttons just a bit more so I can steal another glimpse of what's going on beneath that flimsy piece of fabric. The sweatshirt removal had primed the pump. Most guys look like complete douchebags in plaid shirts. Somehow, Nick pulls it off without looking like a chode.

"My apologies for the lack of furniture. The state of my bank account has convinced me to become a minimalist. So far, I think I've been pretty successful," I say while dramatically opening my arms like I'm trying to sell him this shanty of mine I call home. "But, since I *am* an American, I do have a television. Cable is too rich for my blood, but I have a shit-ton of DVDs piled over yonder if the spirit moves you."

Nick lifts his head, heavily, toward the direction of the pillars of DVDs in the living room. He then staggers away from his post. I'm a little bummed out to see the tension from those buttons released. It takes him a mere three steps to move from the kitchen to the living room. This entire time, I'm silently bitching-out all the sick feces-like stains on the grey carpeting (was it originally white?), but Nick doesn't seem to notice. Thank Christ.

He stands there staring at the piles of DVDs in a silence long enough for a person to take a hearty shit. With a slight raise of his eyebrows, he says, "That's a lot of *Seinfeld*..."

My hand buries itself into the hairline at the base of my skull: a nervous habit I've had for years. "Yeah... I have a thing for Jews."

Nick turns his head to look at me blankly. For a moment I think that I've offended him somehow, but then his laughter breaks the silence. As the intensity of his laughter builds, he squeezes his eyes closed, his body quaking in amusement. One pillar of DVDs collapses as Nick takes a step back while using the knuckle of his pointer finger to wipe away a rogue tear that snuck away. Once he's able to suppress his laughter enough to speak, he says, "That was a weird thing to say." His eyes meet mine, placid pools of unfathomable depth. Water terrifies the shit out of me, but I could swim in those pools for an eternity. Maybe even skinny-dip in them.

A small flutter warms my lower regions.

Shit.

I quickly pull myself out of his gaze, turning my head to the side to look at nothing in particular. If only I had some pictures or some shit on the walls to examine — something to take my mind off of my biological impulses. A portrait of Jesus would be a nice option for visual scrutiny right about now.

I shrug, contorting my face dramatically as I speak. "Hey, what can I say bruh. I'm a shiksa who appreciates a man with a sense of humor. They're

God's people for a reason." Again, my hand weaves itself into the hair just above my neck. Jesus, what do I have to be so nervous about? This is a guy I work with for eight hours or more at a time, five days a week. Our first conversation lasted for hours. What's changed?

What's changed is that you have made it clear as fuckin' day that you want more out of this bromance than someone to make fun of Bobby-Ray Bitches with. He knows that you want his heart, his balls — the entire package.

I'm still unsure of whether Nick shares the same feelings. I mean, he *did* show up for our date. Even though it'd gone in a completely different direction than anticipated, he kept his humor about the circumstances, and it seems like he had fun. But...

...what happens next? Is there some sort of dating protocol that I'm unaware of?

> **Step 1:** set the date to eat food or to see a shitty movie.
> **Step 2:** show up and eat said food/watch said shitty movie.
> **Step 3:** part ways and end the date here, OR continue the evening at one party's residence (continue to step 4).
> **Step 4:** ...

... tha' fuck is **Step 4**!?!?

Before I'm able to figure out what the hell the social protocol calls for, Nick's voice interrupts my anxious pondering. "Is that why you wanted to go out with me? You saw the schnoz and thought I might be an Israelite?" The softness of his eyes and smile tell me he's pulling my leg; there's no way I could offend him. At least around the topic of Judaism.

"Well, you Israeli hot, so... you know." Awkwardly, the right corner of my mouth nervously convulses (there's not better word for it, really) in an attempt to offer a sexy smile. Even though I can't see myself in this moment, I'm sure I look more like Mel Gibson right before an Emmy winning cry than Charlize Theron right before a sex scene. For once, I am at a loss for words. Typically, I have the opposite issue: I don't shut the fuck up. I'm off my game. This lump of graying hamburger floating in my skull has been an endless supply of jokes and sarcasm for as long as I can remember. I got nothing. Shouldn't the booze have given me some sort of confidence boost? I'm bombing. Any moment, a heckler is going to appear and boo me from the stage.

Nick moves his gaze to the floor for a moment, that soft smile complacent and becoming even warmer. He appears to be lost in his own thoughts. Or in the effects of the bitch-booze. Those blonde ringlets of his tumble forward, and I wish I could part those curls and see the thoughts he tucks away so reclusively. What is it that causes him to pause so frequently? Are there painful memories that still sting and sedate? Childhood trauma holding him in place? A lady (or ladies) who tore his heart out and wiped her ass with it?

Am *I* in there somewhere?

Nick lifts his head like he has made a decision. Slowly, he makes his way across the shit-stained carpet, barely missing the heap of DVDs spewed on the floor (what a mood killer it would be for him to fall on his perfect face right now). With each step he takes in my direction, my heart quickens. Every appendage becomes numb. Whether it's from the liquor, lust, or love, I'm not sure.

All my life I've seen moments of love hyperbolized on the screen, through radio speakers, and on the pages of a book (well, only in the books my teachers had forced me to read for class. Lovecraft wasn't one for romance, but you get my point). I'd thought it was all just a crock of shit. Some fluffy idea women had dreamed up to build up the expectations of *all* women to give us hope that we could all experience a love like that someday. Somehow. People, *real* people, couldn't honestly interpret those moments in that dramatized, cliché fashion. Yet, here I am feeling like I'm the protagonist of some corny-as-fuck, poorly written romantic comedy. Here I am playing these moments in slow motion, drinking in every second like I'm a sugar junkie who has never tasted a sweetness of this level.

Here I am paralyzed by passion.

Thoughts and emotions swell within me as Nick stops a mere hand's width in front of me. I can smell the subtle scent of the liquor on his breath mingling with the light cologne he's wearing. A hot iciness suddenly stretches itself over my cheeks, and I raise my head slightly to meet his gaze. We're so close that the honeyed scent of his skin tempts my olfactory receptors.

Harper, keep your shit together. Don't start writing Shakespearian sonnets just yet. You're just two people hanging out. Nothing serious has happened. Chill. Out.

Nick pushes a curtain of red hair behind my ear. The tickle of his finger against my ear sends a chill from my spine to my nipples. Those blue eyes freeze me in place. "You don't know how beautiful you are, do you?"

...well... shit...

Gawking like a kid seeing a paraplegic for the first time, I escape his eyes to glance at the floor briefly. "Well, I've been told that I'm pretty obnoxious."

That was... fucking terrible. Awful. Poorly played, Harper. What are you, thirteen?? He's going to leave. You totally blew it. You need to redeem yourself, quickly.

Before I'm able to clumsily hurl out a vindicating follow-up, Nick wraps his arms around me and pulls me in to meet his lips for the second time this evening. His nose brushes mine, and for a second we share an unseen current. It's so unexpected that my body stiffens at first, but then quickly succumbs to the melting sensation trickling down the front of my chest before pooling around my lady parts. All my regrets, my anxieties, and my shortcomings have vanished. If it were possible, I think I might stay in this moment for the rest of my existence: floating and treading water in a pool of unearthly fantasies. This must be what so many people speak of that I'd originally written off as bullshit.

My hand once again buries itself into a bed of hair. Only this time, it's Nick's. His own hands begin to migrate to the base of my spine, gently infiltrating my sweater and caressing the skin hidden beneath. The sensation of skin-on-skin sends a jolt down the front of my jeans. Nick begins to move forward, guiding me to the mattress on the floor, never parting our lips. We lay there entwined, lips softly saturating one another with much wanted affection. One of Nick's hands smoothes the hair back from my face, glides gently through its length, and then tip-toes down each of my vertebra.

I allow my own hands to wander. My palms begin to journey against his chest. Soon after, one tip-toes down his front. It glides down, making a slight turn before slipping between the waist of his jeans and hip. My open palm swoops in a half-moon toward his inner thigh, gently grazing the soft hair framing the part that I'm really after. The part that tiny trail of happiness had highlighted for me earlier like a sexy appetizer.

Suddenly, Nick's lips stop moving. His hands freeze and then abandon my shirt. Sternly, but not forcibly, he pulls my hand from its intrusion. After a slight pause, I feel him braid his fingers between my own. I open my eyes.

The fuck just happened?

*You moved too fast—you moved too fast—you moved too fast. Blew it. Good-bye, any chance of falling in love with **a nice guy**. Adios.*

Nick opens his own eyes, meeting my gaze. There's a sadness beneath the adoration. "I think we should stop. We've been drinking, and I don't want to ruin this by jumping into things too quickly." He brings my hand to his lips and gives it an affectionate kiss. "Could we maybe take things slow?"

I kick all of my lady fantasies out of view and spring out of my euphoria. "Yeah, sure. You brought up *Seinfeld*, started to talk about Jews, and it got me all hot and bothered. My sincerest apologies."

The joke lands; Nick laughs.
Sweet vindication.

"Well, I'm partly at fault, too. When I saw the two six-foot-tall stacks of Jewish comedy, I should have known something was amiss." The smile he sends makes me feel like I could conquer Mt. Washington in the nude with my tits tied behind my back. That smile said what words could never say and told me everything I needed to hear. It said, "I adore the shit out of you even if you make horrible jokes. I'd still buy tickets to your show and would throat-punch the hecklers."

I wrap my arms around Nick's shoulders innocently and shrug my own. "Meh, that's a lesson learned, right?" That smile of his warms, and then Nick leans in to gift me with another kiss while I try my best to keep my lady parts from overheating. Do they make some kind of coolant for the clitoris? Never have I wanted to fuck a person so badly, but I know Nick's right. We should take things slow. I'd grown so accustomed to guys prioritizing that aspect of relations that I'd assumed that this was **Step 4** to the dating protocol. I've also never been so emotionally and physically attracted to a person, so I'd become lost in the moment. Thank God, Nick seemed to have had become lost himself and things aren't awkward.

He rests his forehead against mine, pinning a few of his curls between us. "We should probably try to get some sleep. Tomorrow we have a full shift. That means at least four hours of DJ Booty Stank," he says, his voice low.

"Oh God, I'll need plenty of rest and patience for them sick beats." I hesitate for a moment and then grab one last kiss. I nuzzle my face into his chest, holding him closer. "Good night, Nick."

"Good night, Harper…" These words mixed with the sound of his heartbeat are the lullaby that carries me off to sleep.

Chapter 18

A Blue Christmas

Christmas is that time of year where life has reached the highest peak of shittiness, yet we mash it together with this season of love and giving. It's like we've tricked ourselves as a society to think that this time of year isn't actually death in its purest essence, but is instead one of the happiest times of year. The days are growing shorter, which means more darkness and less overall productivity. I've heard people say they sleep a lot during the winter. Oh, boo-fuckin'-hoo. Not only do I become sluggishly miserable during this annual period of death called winter, but my pussy-wussy fear of the dark causes me to sleep even *less* during the winter months, resulting in my depression and overall quality of life to plummet into the icy asshole of seasonal despair...

...and then I think about how cushy my life must be that such an expected, natural change in my surroundings makes me sad and that it's in fact a widely accepted "condition" (SAD: Seasonal Affective Disorder — yup). These are tough times we live in...

But oh, there's ***Christmas***!

It's the season for **giving**. What this translates to, when you're a cynical prick like me, is that it's the season for **commerce**. Feeling the sadness of reality? Go buy your dad a meat log adorned with a variety of cheeses and forget about that growing sense of insignificance! Buy yourself blind! Go sing some vomit inducing music — who gives a shit if you can sing or if you've heard it a thousand times since breakfast — or buy (**buy-buy-buy**) a festive tie! Oh, and don't forget about seasonal coffee flavors! They're seasonal flavors because we said so. **Fuck you; it's Christmas.**

You know, I used to love Christmas. It was a magical time of year when kindness and good cheer were practiced. People were **nice**. The warmth and generosity made the falling temperatures outside bearable. As I get older, there's less and less of this warm generosity. People only become more impersonal. More bitter. Less kind. Christmas goodies overthrow the Halloween merchandise before anyone has even had a chance to take their kids trick-or-treating. Every year, my level of pissed off-itry elevates as I see more and more of this useless shit put onto the shelves while our country sinks more and more into debt. Countless ceramic Santas smile back at shoppers with twinkling eyes, not even a bit worried about the pounds upon pounds of cookies and Christmas fudge shifting their pancreata into overdrive, slowly turning them into diabetics. Symbolism, or what? Sometimes I wonder if it's society that's becoming colder or whether it's, in fact, myself.

The gentle twinkling of jingle bells approaches from behind me, giggling rhythmically, and soon Megan makes her way behind the black countertop. The nails of her finely manicured hands have tiny candy canes etched onto them (painted? I have no idea how the hell nails are done; I gnaw my own raw before they've even had a chance to see the daylight). Pearly white snowflakes hang from her ears and a touch of green shadow frames her warm eyes. The contrast is captivating to the point that I *almost* start to question my sexuality. Almost. Christmas might have an embellished tradition of money circulation, but at least people like Megan get to wear cute little Santa hats and festively coordinate their outfits, accessories, and makeup. These little things bring happiness to some people, and happiness and joy are crucial to surviving this darkening world. Who am I to determine the worth of happiness even if it's gained through false realities?

Fuck you; it's Christmas.

Megan leans against the counter with her hip, crossing her arms. Her green apron is covered in holiday themed pins advertising the deals of the season. That poor, undeserving apron has more flair than Owen Wilson with a cold. Despite the snowmen guzzling gourmet espresso beverages (okay, how does this make sense??? The coffee would surely destroy the snowmen from the inside out. It would be like watching a person drink sulfuric acid or a seasonal adaptation of *Alien*) wired onto her front, Megan still manages to look beautiful. Of course. Why wouldn't she? I've yet to see this chick look anything less than flawless. Anytime I wear anything even remotely tacky, I look silly and jester-like (well, I guess that *is* my role) while Megan somehow makes it sexy. Life isn't fair sometimes, am I right?

"I'll be *so* happy once Christmas is over. I know most of the time I complain about how boring the night shift can be, but the types of families who do their Christmas shopping at night are *so* weird." Megan brings a hand to her temple, reminding me of the Grinch bitching about all of the noise-noise-noise from atop his lonely mountain. That is, if the Grinch were a sexy barista in the city. Now, *there's* a television drama: *Sexy Barista in the City*. So much caffeine-fueled sexy time.

I make an exaggerated sound, like someone just kicked me in the uterus, as I jump up to park my keister onto the counter. "Aw, come on. They can't be *that* weird. I totally understand why someone would shop at night. Less people and shit to deal with. I prefer my strategy, personally: don't go Christmas shopping. It saves me a world of stress and financial anguish."

Megan rolls her eyes. "Jesus, you have to like Christmas at least a *little* bit, Harper. It gives people an excuse to buy people presents and to eat sugar." To demonstrate her point, she grabs a holiday bar (I think the cranberries are what makes it "holiday") out of the bakery case and takes a bite. How can she eat with lipstick on? Wait a minute — will I *finally* get to see Megan with some type of flaw, even if it's a measly cosmetic smudgery? Of course, I know that this would never be. She probably uses some kind of Manhattan Project lipstick that could withstand a meteor crashing to the earth. ***My friends are all dead, but damn, don't my lips look killer!?***

She lightly brushes the crumbs from her lips. No smudges.

...Bitch...

I arch my back and push out my gut as far as I can. With both hands, I then proceed to give it a good rub down. "I admit that the ugly sweaters are a great hide-away for my winter fudge-pudge, but the shopping pressures... And it's sort of like a month-long reminder that you're alone."

I've never admitted to this aspect of my cynical view on Christmas, not even to myself. This is the first year that I'll be spending the holidays without my parents or childhood friends. This is the first year I'll spend trapped inside of my painfully empty apartment. I'm really not sure why I so casually shared this with a person I'd known for less than a year, but there it was. The reaction I'd been expecting was one of sarcasm or snotty disagreement. Maybe even her signature eye roll.

Instead, Megan's features soften and fall. There's a moment of quiet thought and then she offers, "Hey, you have Nick, right?" Her features again lift, brightening her face like the first candlelight during a power outage. It's both comforting and encouraging, reminding me that darkness is temporary. At some point, even in Alaska, the sun does shine again.

She's got you there, friend.

Even before this life-altering, bitch-you-crazy move to the city, I'd never spent this time of giving with a sweetheart. Will and I were still only a few months into our "dating" status for that first Christmas, and he hadn't survived long enough for us to have a second. Yeah, I know that I had parents to share most of the holidays with during my pre-South Harbor days, and I know that not every person has had the privilege of seeing colorful gifts waiting under a decked-out evergreen on Christmas morning, but there's something unique about "romantic" love. Family *has* to love you. They may not like you, but they have to love you. There are biological impulses, societal expectations, and even some laws (who wants DHS on their ass?) that demand your family love you. With romantic love, the other party is *choosing* to love you. Okay, so really pathetic hopeless romantics might argue, "Oh, you can't choose who you love!" Alright, this might be, but they don't **have** to pursue you. They don't **have** to keep you around. And they don't just keep you around because they don't want the neighbors to talk shit or to keep the cops out of their biz. They keep you around because the **want** you around.

Plus, this type of love allows a level of intimacy that's illegal to share with family (in most states, anyway).

In my lovesick stupor, I'd apparently started to smile like that person at the party who has had far too much Molly and has now made friends with the household cat. After feeling my slack jawed expression on my stupid face, I regain my composure and straighten my posture. The playful reveal of Megan's pearly whites from behind her crumb-less lipstick tells me that she has caught me during this moment of weakness.

"Yeah, I guess you're right. I do have a hot piece of man meat to spend the holidays with." I tighten my lips and inhale dramatically like I'd just stubbed my pinky toe on the coffee table for the 1,000,000,000,000,000th time.

Megan throws her head back in laughter, the bells on her corny-as-cow-shit hat jingling in sync with each spasm. She places one hand on the counter and the other on an extended hip, leaning toward me like she's about to tell me the confidentially hidden truth of the Kennedy assassination.

Lowering her chin slightly, she peers up at me, her caramel eyes bubbling with interest. "So, how's that going, any way? You never really talk about it much. Is he treating you alright? Got any spicy stories to tell?" She casually leans against the counter with a hip, waiting patiently for my answer. But I can tell there's no use in trying to deter her. Somehow, she always manages to get answers. I still can't tell whether I consistently cave because she's just so damn insistent, or if deep down I really do want to discuss all this mooshy-gooshy bullshit with someone.

My money's on the latter.

Fuck off.

Placing my hands behind me, I lean back slightly. I'm trying my best to appear cool and confident even though I feel like a Mormon in a dildo shop. "Well, Megan my dear, I'm not one to kiss and tell, but he's a sweet guy. You were right about him being one of the nice ones, so thanks for that. He's one of the few people who seems to get my constant sarcasm and can spend more than a few hours around me without wanting to dig his eardrums out with dirty spoons."

There. That was an answer, a damn fine one...
... apparently, it's not fine enough for Megan.

One of her perfectly groomed brows raises slightly, insisting on more details. "Of course I was right. Jesus, it was so obvious." She puffs out an annoyed breath like I'd just asked her if *The Hunger Games* is based on a true story. "So, has he taken you anywhere nice? Has he done anything cute for you?"

"When your first for-realz date is to a strip club, it's sort of hard to top that level of class. Mostly we just hang out at cost-free places. Who needs to blow a bunch of cash on someone they've already won over?"

"Sure, whatever. Have you had sex yet?" The blunt casualness of her question hits me right in the gut, stealing the wind from my lungs, and for a moment I forget to breathe. I'm trying to determine whether she had seriously just asked me such a personal question.

"The fuck, Megan. Why would you ask me something like that?" Is this just how girls talk now? Am I *that* pathetic, or has it been that long since I've had a girlfriend and/or had sex? Was it a combination of these factors mashed into a disgusting lump of self-consciousness?

God, I'm lame. Like captain of the math team lame.

There it is: Megan's signature eyeroll. "Oh, come on Harper. Don't be such a prude. Everyone has sex, so spill it." I can't tell whether her lack of shame around this very personally intimate subject is appalling or admirable. There are no signs of discomfort or embarrassment in her expression. She simply stands waiting, hand still on that outward hip, as if she had asked me what my favorite film was (**not** *Scarface*, thank you very much). Why had sex become such an uncomfortable topic for me? Well, I guess that isn't *entirely* true. I make sex jokes *almost* as frequently as I make fart jokes. It's a close second, really, in my repertoire. I've even combined the two to make wonderfully disgusting jokes about Brazilian Fart-Porn from time to time. Once the discussion becomes directly related to me is when I slam that door closed and force its deadbolt in place. We all know how well I've got that door-locking routine down.

When did I become so sexually awkward? Was it due to lack of experience? Was it due to the fact that so many people with a Y chromosome were interested in that part of my person but nothing more? Am I so "prude" out of resentment? The few occasions that I did bump uglies with someone were mechanical and unfulfilling. There was no passion, no connection. No love. Nick had been the first person I've ever "made a move" on and he quickly, but politely, had passed on the invitation. Okay, so I guess it was more like a rain check than a complete pass. His reasoning had made sense to me at the time, so I didn't get too upset about it, but...

The waiting is becoming intolerable.

Every touch of his fingers, every union of bare skin drives my ovaries closer and closer to bursting in anticipation. And oh — those eyes. Don't get me started on those mesmerizing globes. Those things truly test my constitution. Was it possible to die from an overdose of horniness? Hey, I guess I'll be the first person to find out! Maybe I can donate my unused sex organs to science.

As much as I care about Nick and adore his personality, I don't think a completely abstinence-based relationship would work. Intimacy of the flesh can be the ultimate form of expressing love, and I want to discover how beautiful it could really be.

It feels like society is beginning to slowly shift its view on love and sex, as Megan so frankly demonstrated. I always found it odd that violence is so accepted, yet anything remotely sexual is still sometimes hidden. You can show her boobies, but I'll be damned if there's a nipple involved! Oh, you want to broadcast a bunch of sweaty, tights-wearing dudes pretending to hit each other and hurling scripted insults? Sounds great! Sure, teach our children about the Trail of Tears and the horrors of the Holocaust, but for the love of the sweet baby Jesus, do NOT teach them how the reproductive system works! That will only put the idea of sex into their heads. By that same logic, wouldn't teaching kids about Adolf Hitler and the Nazi Party create tiny little neo-Nazis? That logic is so flawed. Sex, an act that can be out of love, is so shunned when it should instead at least be acknowledged. **This is coming from a complete prude!** But, at the same time, since sex has the potential to be so spiritually satisfying, I do still strongly believe that one should not hand themselves out like SAMs Club coupons.

Anyway, enough of that sappy shit...

I look toward the paper snowflakes hanging from the ceiling (is that gum? impressive...) and think of how to answer this diddy of an inquiry. "No, no intercourse yet. Close, but no cigar, Sally." Remembering my icy coffee with the unconscionable amount of chocolate sauce, I snatch it up. I'm sure to sip from it as loudly as possible. Maybe the disgusting noises will be so loud, Megan will only be able to focus on how much of a disgusting slob I am rather than my obligatory chastity.

The annoying antic doesn't seem to attract any of Megan's attention; her mouth is gaping when I look back in her direction, a slightly puzzled expression on her face. Her hand abandons her hip and relocates to her temple (all of the **noise-noise-noise**). She looks the way I feel when I'm around small children or when I hear people excitedly recounting what happened on the latest episode of *Jimmy Fallon Live*. "You haven't had sex yet!? Seriously? How long have you two been seeing each other? Like, three months? That's practically half a year!" On the last syllable, her hand flicks outward, trying to knock away the absurdity of my answer.

I feel myself getting slightly defensive at her response. "Yeah, so what? I'm sure there are still people who don't fuck until they are married. What the hell is a few months? Are you saying you and that guy you're seeing, D-Bag, have already been bruising the beef-curtains?"

Yeah, Mormons don't fuck until they are married. In some cultures, couples do the Dirty Tango through a hole in a sheet. That gonna be you?

Megan's free hand finds its way back to her hip and she cocks her head slightly. "Most people have sex within the first couple of months, Harper. And his name is D-Black. Some people don't even date. They just screw. Find someone to have sex with, no strings attached. What do you think Tinder is? *A dating app*??" Once again, the hand abandons the hip and then cradles an invisible scrotum in a "no shit" gesture.

Not wanting to spill my diabetes-inducing beverage, I place my coffee cup beside me and pull a leg further onto the counter so I can turn to face Megan more directly. "I don't subscribe to that. Tinder or that line of thought. Yeah, what people do is totally their call. They can fuck garbage disposals for all I care. And yeah, sex isn't this disgusting act that society made it out to be in the past. It's not gross or immoral, and being promiscuous doesn't label a person as a 'bad' human being. BUT – it's still a big deal. How can anyone argue that letting another person shove a body part into his or her orifice, or orifices, isn't a big deal? Penetration means that person is *literally* inside of you. How the fuck is that not a big deal?!" The air around me has been heated by the frustrated blood that's boiled up to my cheeks. Maybe I freaked out a little bit, but seriously, this whole loose sexual attitude (yeah, the word choice was intentional) of people my age drives me fucking insane.

For a moment, Megan freezes. I can see her eyes spinning with thought. I can't tell whether I've offended her, or if the flipping of my shit caused her to re-evaluate some of her life choices. Or both. Some of the color drains away from her face and her eyes haze over.

Shit, I had to open my mouth...
That's me: the social assassin.

I'm sure that my thoughts on sex, like my thoughts on Christmas, are of the minority. Yeah, I could argue that the majority of the German population adored Adolf Hitler, but something as harmless as sex (if we look at the big picture, right?) isn't the type of thing to get all preachy about. This is one of those **situations** where I need to just swallow my stupid, stubborn pride and accept that I'm the minority.

A shaky breath escapes me, and I bring my other leg to the counter. I face Megan full on. "Look, I'm sorry for freakin' out like a little bitch. It's just all of these societal norms and pressures get to me. Just because I have a different opinion than the majority,

I'm automatically weirder than a vegan in a steakhouse." I pause, debating whether to continue. I've said this much already; there's no sense in holding back. I close my eyes, embracing darkness for the first time ever. I can't bear to make eye contact while sharing this confession. "Maybe deep down I feel like sex should be an expression of love, and maybe — just maybe — this is based on unsuccessful experiences." The lids of my eyes open cautiously, and I await the ridicule surely to follow. Instead, I'm greeted by kindness in those caramel eyes.

That nomadic hand lays itself over her heart. "Oh, Harper, I knew you had a heart in there." She flutters her feathery lashes playfully.

"Fuck off." I can't help but laugh. She zinged me.

Megan hops that tight little booty of hers onto the counter beside me. We probably look like two fifteen-year-old girls at a slumber party having a heated conversation about how cute Johnny Jockstrap is. She glances at the floor for a moment, and then the gentle interrogation begins again. "So, if you've had only unsuccessful sexual experiences and you feel the way you do, you didn't love any of those guys, right?" She waits with a cordial patience that invites confidence, but doesn't demand it.

"Nope. Guess not." There's no hesitation in my answer, which causes my chest to ache with guilt over Will. I've got to be the worst human being to grace God's green Earth. I'm so sorry.

After giving an appropriate amount of "wait time" that would make a schoolteacher proud, Megan asks, "Well, do you love Nick?" Again, she sits quiet and receptive like I'm the only person in the universe, and all of her time is mine to use as needed.

Again, there's no hesitation. "Yeah, I do love him." This is the first time I've admitted this aloud. It felt sort of good, almost like taking a dump after days of irritating constipation. From the day I met him, I think I knew that I was in love with him. It was only recently that I allowed myself to put a label on these feelings. Once you slap that label on, there's no quick removal. It's like when you use those cheap Do-it-Yourself glue on nails. At first, you appreciate the simple beauty of the things, but once they begin to get irritating and you decide that they really aren't working out, the removal seems impossible. You scrape, and prod, and curse, or you end up using some vile smelling chemicals to dissolve them away. Either way, it never ends well, and it's enough to make you never want to try it again.

(Alright, Harper, calm down with the metaphors.)

But, I can't lie to myself anymore about the way I feel about Nick. Sharing this with another person made it feel more real and even more special, if that makes sense.

The bells on her Santa hat cough lightly as Megan gives a slight nod. "So, why haven't you tried with him yet?" Megan's method of coaxing out information is like having a beautiful therapist who smells of the sweet scent of coffee beans. (...*okay, so I guess there are more metaphors to be had...*) The Zen tone and the sympathy in her voice hypnotically convinces your own vocal chords to start working before your mind is even aware that it had a thought inside of it, let alone that it had spoken.

I snort and give an annoyed laugh. "At the end of our first real date, I tried to get things going. Nick stopped it and basically said he didn't want to move too fast. Said he was afraid it might ruin things." Saying this out loud to another person made it sound like the stupidest fucking excuse ever even though it'd sounded so reasonably rational in the moment. Kind of like trying to help people save money by forcing them to pay for health care that they can't even afford. The liquor could've had something to do with my initial interpretation, or my sexual frustration could have something to do with my current analysis. Who knows? Megan, perhaps?

As soon as I'd repeated the lame-ass excuse my curly-headed Romeo had given me, Megan's face softens and brightens. She looks like just saw the cutest puppy on the planet playing with a tiny baby goat. She places her hand on her heart once again. "That is so freakin' cute!"

Hmm. Maybe it wasn't a shitty excuse, after all. But...

"Know what's not cute? Having a horrid case of blue bean for two months straight." I take an angry sip from my coffee, scowling. I don't mean just a "I'm a little mad" or "I disprove of your actions" frown. I was straight up scowling. Hardcore.

I hadn't intended for this to be a joke, but Megan takes a moment to enjoy laughing at my expense. One of her hands covers her mouth to try to stop the onslaught. She's able to quiet herself and says, "Alright, but have you tried again since then? It *has* been a little while. Maybe he will be ready this time?" Megan offers while letting her hand drop to her lap.

Hmm.
Interesting prospect.

CHAPTER 19
DANGER ZONE

It is a wintry Saturday night; Harper and I are in her apartment watching a movie.

We are snuggling each other tightly on her (hopefully) coffee stained loveseat. The stain had actually been made prior to our acquiring it off the side of the road one afternoon while driving by a clothes-littered alleyway just down the road from a recent job. With crude cardboard signs duct taped to half of the miscellaneous pile of stuff, clearly, someone had either been evicted or caught cheating on his/her spouse. Either way, it meant a free couch for Harper. We strapped it to the top of the Lumina with the dozens of bungee cords I keep in the trunk and took off into the sunset. Nothing says I love you like the gift of an abandoned dumpster loveseat.

The first inklings of snow start to rake and tap against the fog stained windows of her dimly lit apartment. With nothing but the technicolor shadows of her TV illuminating the dark confines of the room, the night feels slow and preserved as if time had been dipped in molasses. Sitting here with her wrapped adoringly in my arms feels so right that I wish this moment would never end. Her fragrant hair wafts under my breath and tickles my chin as I cradle and rock her in my arms with nothing but warm love radiating outward, sealing us in a feeling of ultimate loving divinity. With her doll like fingers wrapped in mine, we sit quietly and watch *Top Gun* as the monstrous grey clouds rolling and creeping over the pounding ocean current shed their molecularly frozen skin across the soon to be sleeping city.

We have both seen the movie before multiple times, but never together. We talked at work about how awesomely bad it was, and when I brought it in one night for her to borrow, she insisted I come over and watch it with her later. I figured that I was safe due to the extremely gay undertones of the entire film and saw no harm in viewing it privately with her. No overly erotic sex scenes to spark the mood; just deliciously hilarious pseudo-masculine dialogue over cheesy, recycled 80's music. As Tom Cruise is just arriving to the academy and is forcing himself on an older, attractive lady in a bar by displaying his super manly knowledge of show tunes, I feel movement down around my crotch. Slowly, I hear my front zipper being undone and the feeling of tiny, wriggling fingers around my lower tummy. Instinctively, my hands go to my pants, and I find Harper's delicate fingertips eagerly trying to work the rest of the zipper down on my tight denim jeans.

"So much for a surprise," she breathes to me with some nervous lust in her voice, and she then proceeds to venture farther. In one fluid motion, I pull her hand out and re-zip my pants before sitting up. Harper lays back against the other side of the seat and watches me with much interest until she realizes that I am not taking my pants off. Desperately trying to save the moment, she seductively takes off her shirt and leggings, tossing them onto the floor behind the couch.

I stare in amazement at the fine goosebumps forming across her tight, glistening skin illuminated by the dull glow of the television. Her smooth legs part ever so slightly to tease me with glimpses of her frilly pink panties that don't at all match the loosely fitting bra that she starts to slide off her elegantly angled shoulders, soon joining the other garments behind the couch. My pants become tighter and tighter with each passing moment, and as she reaches out and grabs one of my members through the rough material of my jeans, I panic at how to go forward. Having found Lefty, she methodically starts to rub up and down the bulging shaft forming on my thigh, her rhythm strong but gentle in pressure. I am praying she doesn't explore the other leg to find Righty when the brilliant idea hits me.

"Lay back," I say trying to muster a false bravado in my dry, toneless voice. She looks shyly into me for only a second before obeying, draping herself back over the arm of the couch while I move to the floor and confidently spread her legs open. I then gently pull her panties off, careful not to knock my elbows off the coffee table behind me, and proceed to kiss the hot skin of her inner right thigh.

Eyes closed, I work my tongue and lips up and down her silky inner thighs before gently kissing her throbbing clit. Framed by her moist, shaven lips, glowing and blushing like two sun baked rose petals as my rough, wet tongue laps and glides across every gap and crevice. She quivers longingly at my touch, and soon her legs come down and wrap delicately around my shoulders as my hands drift up to her tender breasts, kneading and tenderly groping them. Working her nipples and clit at the same time, I can feel her constitution becoming malleable like warm putty in my strong, strangely confident hands. Every pass of my sharp, tapered tongue combined with every pinch from my greedy fingers was gradually liquefying her, sending her to a state of pure unabashed ecstasy.

The confusing sounds of poorly written (always gay) fake Air Force lingo fills the air around my ears as my mind and mouth blindly go to work at mapping out the coordinates of the various slits and curves of her petite pussy. Her freshly shaven skin against my nose and cheeks feels like the prickly softness of a fresh Georgia peach newly picked from an ancient family orchard. My greedy hands only leave her supple breasts long enough to momentarily hold her legs back so I can push my puckered mouth deeper into her moist hole, instantly feeling her insides tightening in surprised response around my wriggling, pink tongue. I gently nibble on the end of her clit, suckling softly in between rough, animalistic kisses; her sweet, juicy nectar dripping down my chin.

With her legs wrapped around my head now, I can feel her pushing against every stroke and lash of my wet, bumpy tongue. Her thighs bracingly start to clamp down on my skull as I free my right hand and slide a single finger inside of her. She gasps, kicking out with her legs and knocking a glass loudly off the coffee table behind me. I make to try to pick up the broken cup down by my feet, but Harper grabs me by the hair and says furtively, "No. Don't stop," and guides me back down to where I passionately kiss her sticky cookie and immediately get back to work.

With my mouth sucking and licking at her in every conceivable way, Harper convulses wildly on the arm of the couch as if she is having a full-blown epileptic seizure. Eyes rolled backwards and hands knotted painfully in my hair, I instinctively know these are the signs of the mystical and elusive female orgasm. I went into this last-minute plan of fellatio thinking that my chances of getting her to cum were 50/50. Now I can see that this is a home run.

Feeling like Picasso, I paint an epic picture with my tongue that could only be seen psycho-connectedly through means of sexual osmosis. Each pass of the rough side followed by a circular swirl from the lubed, slick side of my masterful tongue is sending waves of explosive energy up and down her strenuously taut muscles and twitching spine. Sensing the final moments approaching, I motorboat her hot, throbbing bean and go for the gold.

She can only fight the moaning and screaming for so long before bursting into hysterical fits of growling, yelping pleasure. I soon feel her slim fingers lock into my crown of curls, forming an iron fist, ruggedly pulling my face deeper into her with complete, lustful abandonment.

The heat coming off her inner thighs warmly stings my face, raising beads of perspiration that swell with the ever-nearing orgasm that is slowly building up inside of her. I quicken my pace now, tongue flying in and around her fun button, while I listen to her lose herself in this moment of complete alternate perceptions where even one's own identity gets lost in the thick haze of self-projected pleasures and inner desires. The fist in my hair twists to a painful snarl and acts as a clear signal for me to go faster and deeper. Our bodies grind and gyrate in unison until a mighty quake rocks through Harper's tiny, shaky frame, causing her to almost knee me right in the nose as I am trying to escape her ever tightening leg lock around my head.

I glance up in time to see her flushed face, her eyes now tiny slits filled with nothing but pure white. A free hand grabs at her sweat glistened body as if she might convulse and quiver herself into a million pieces. Gasping for air and slowly coming back from that dimensionless cavern of pure white light that temporarily blinds us all when in the throes of ultimate sexual enlightenment, she shakily leans forward and kisses me on the cheek with scarlet, blood filled lips.

"I love you, Nick," she whispers. She then moans in a mix of effort and lingering pleasure as she leans back against the couch and takes a moment to collect herself.

I hear this from miles away. Never before had I been so emotionally intertwined with anyone on such a molecular level. In the most intense moments of our lustful bondage, I completely forgot about that metaphorical double-sided wall that separates us from ever being together. When she spoke those four words to me, I knew that she meant them. Hearing them out loud was somehow terrifying and spellbinding at the same time. How can my worst nightmare and my deepest fantasies be the same scenario? Well, almost the same. In the deep Utopian dreams, I am a real boy, not this miscarved freak fashioned with too many wooden legs. Sure, she loves me now, but once she sees my twin peaks, I doubt she will ever be able to look at me this way again. And so goes my life. Enjoy the moment, Nick, while you still can.

"I love you, too," I finally say with slippery, numb lips.

I lazily wash and wipe off my face with a towel

from the bathroom. I sit back down on the couch next to her just in time to watch Tom Cruise and Val Kilmer play sweaty, half-naked volleyball while the very heterosexual music of the late and great Kenny Loggins scores over every poorly edited spike and serve. Harper gets up long enough to grab a blanket off the back of the couch, wrapping it tightly around herself as she snuggles tightly into me.

As we both drifted off to sleep with visions of unnecessarily close male locker room arguments and unintentionally funny double entendres disguised as Hollywood tough guy rhetoric, a calm misted and accumulated with fog throughout the room. With a slight smile on my sweat stained face, I sit back and run my fingers through her long red hair as I watch the director try desperately to give the audience the impression that Tom Cruise isn't standing on orange crates during all his kissing scenes.

As my eyelids grow heavy and I start to dissolve back to that shapeless void of borderless nothing and mesmerizing scenes trapped behind translucent windows, Goose is breaking his neck as Maverick ejects them from the failing fighter jet as it careens into the wide-open sea. Ultimately, Maverick's lack of caution and respect for others costs the life of his crew member and best friend, a haunting memory that drives him to be the best pilot in the academy until a short time later where he is simply over that biz and oddly tosses Goose's dog tags carelessly into the ocean.

Somewhere, way back in the deep, razor-thin cracks that cover the back walls of the shadowy recesses of my mind, I would like to think that this ominous scene isn't lost on me. For you see, just like Goose, I am putting my young, hopeful life in the hands of a giant, unempathetic dick(s) whose reckless and unorthodox rejection of society's social standards will inevitably be my own undoing.

Chapter 20

A Festivus Miracle

For Christmas Eve, the weather is pretty mild and unusually comfortable. Actually, it's pretty damn nice out. One might say that it's a beautiful winter's day. But, I'm not that someone. I still abhor winter, but I'll admit that today *is* pretty nice. There's still a little bit of that winter nip in the air, but my lungs don't feel like they're being pumped full of liquid nitrogen every time I breathe. I also appreciate the fact that the air isn't cold enough to cause my teeth to throb with pain, either. In Maine, I've learned that Winter is a cruel mistress. I've probably heard the story about the ice storm of 1990 something about fifty times (so, *how* many days was it that you didn't have running water? Cheese-and-rice, how *did* you **survive**!). So, I assume that I've been incredibly lucky this winter. So far. I'm sure that at some point soon she will spread her cheeks and defecate that icy shit all over us, but I'll enjoy the weather while I can.

The city is practically empty. Very few cars pollute the streets, so it's quiet. Some might say *serene*. Today is the last hoo-rah before Santa squeezes his buttery buns through all the kids' chimneys, so all the shop fronts are decorated to their maximum capacities. Even *Lloyd's Laundromat*, a scuzzy place with three poorly running machines that I swear is just a front for a drug dealer, has silvery snowflakes twinkling from the one tiny (cracked?) window. There's even a soft snow shower floating down from above, polka dotting my clothes and hair.

How thematic.

Nick and I'd decided to spend Christmas Eve together. I was a little shy (*awkward-cowardly*) about inviting him over for a festively romantic evening, so I instead mentioned that we might as well take advantage of our night off together to hang out at my place. It just happened to be that it was Christmas Eve is all. No big thing, ya' know? No pressure.

Yeah, no pressure, but you would have howled in disappointment as your mascara ran into a pint of Ben and Jerry's, cursing yourself in self-pity at the fact that you were alone on some commercialized holiday, if he had declined. Hypocrite.

Of course, he'd seen right through my pathetic farce and agreed to spend the night at my place.

When Nick got to my place, I'd expected him to

try to take me out to dinner to make up for our first failed dinner attempt so many months ago. Typical, but thoughtful... I guess. Instead, he'd given me two twenties and asked me to go get a coffee and our Christmas Eve dinner. When I'd asked him why he wanted me to go alone, his response was, "Nunya' business." Okay, so he said it in his sweet, sophisticated Nick way, but that was the basic message. Two in the afternoon is a little early for dinner, but with the shrinking amount of daylight and a sunset time of approximately three o'clock (being the state with the first sunrise means it also has the first sunset, mind you), I think the early dinnertime was intentional. I don't think Nick has caught on to my childlike fear of the dark yet, but walking alone at night during the months of winter can be balls-cold.

What **a nice guy**.

What Nick didn't realize is that his request for me to evacuate my living quarters actually did me a solid, too. I had a gift for him (come on, I'm not *that* shitty of a girlfriend), but I had nothing to wrap it with. I know I'm lame and cynical, but I still wanted to have *some* sort of packaging or wrapping to clothe it with. Receiving a naked Christmas present is even lamer than my outlook on the holidays.

Oh, please. You're not fooling anyone...

Okay, fine. I admit that tonight will be the first Christmas spent with a boyfriend. Not only is it unique in that way, but I'll be spending my first holiday with the first person I've ever cared about in that Nicholas Sparks/Jane Austen way. I didn't understand that stupid phrase, "he gives me butterflies in my stomach" (what, he gives you gas?) until I met Nick. Anytime I just *think* about the guy, there's a kaleidoscope of butterflies flapping around in my gut, crashing into each other every which way like a flock of drunken teenagers. Yeah, I know that Nick and I've never officially labeled what we have as a relationship or christened one another as our boyfriend or girlfriend, but that seems like such a contrived thing to do. What do people do? Do they say, "My lady, this evening was quite enchanting; what do you say we go steady, mmm?" or, "Hey, wanna be my boyfran?" Get the fuck out of here.

Maybe that's why so many people feel compelled to have such a strong cyber presence. All of that awkward, real-life shit can be done behind the safety of a screen. Do people even break-up in "real life" anymore, or does one partner simply set his/her status as "single" on Facebook? It's fine that Nick hasn't officially claimed me as his lady. The insects fluttering around in my gut are enough to tell me that what we have is suh-en special.

After stopping by my coffee place to grab the worst latte that has ever disgraced my lips (**fuck you, Damien...**), I grabbed a gift bag from the dollar store while I waited for our Chinese food (what else would we order on Christmas Eve?). With Nick's gift hidden within the belly of the blue, snowflake adorned bag hanging from the crook of my elbow and the Chinese food in one hand and *Festive Fecal Latte* (patent pending) in the other, I made my way back to my apartment.

I wonder what the sneaky bastard has been up to?

***

"I've come bearing Chinese food!" I hold the plastic bag of MSG-infused goodness out like the finest bottle of imported merlot. I almost spill my coffee in the process. It wouldn't have been much of a loss (**seriously, _fuck you_, Damien**...), but how awful would it be to have even *more* shit stains on the carpet? The apartment is dim, and I realize that the lights are off. The sun hasn't quite set, but it's still well beyond the "lights-on" time of day.

Nick looks up at me from the comfort of my curbside loveseat. His eyes are electrified under the glowing pattern of colors softly illuminating the living room. The delicate colors dance between the fine stubble of his unshaven cheeks. "God bless the Chinese for operating their businesses, no matter the holiday. Bring it in here."

I'm still not quite sure what Nick's been up to, but I obey his request. At first, I assume that he has set up a tiny and/or fake Christmas tree in the living room for us to gaze upon as we stuff our faces with greasy food. Typical Christmas shit for a twenty-something-year-old, right? Once I step into the living room far enough (about six to ten paces) to see where the lights are coming from, I just stand there gawking in disbelief.

There, in the corner of my hobbit-sized living room, is a plain aluminum pole wrapped in multi-colored lights. Comically, there are only enough of the tiny multicolored lights to wrap around about half of the pole. A small box wrapped in brown paper rests against it.

This is probably the most beautiful thing I've ever laid my eyes upon.

Nick flashes a red carpet worthy smile and says, "Happy Festivus, Harper."

I'm stunned. Yeah, it sounds stupid, but this is the most thoughtful thing anyone has ever done for me. The holidays are so formulaic and commercialized that I've grown to hate the triteness of them. Somehow, Nick found a way to celebrate the holidays together in way that made it special for me again. Most chicks probably want a fancy homemade dinner or a dozen roses waiting for them. At least that's what pop culture has led me to believe. The aluminum pole in my living room was better than anything I could've expected. Everyone knows that obsessive *Seinfeld* nerd. The person who quotes the sitcom at least once per day (there's a *Seinfeld* episode for every situation of life, I swear to Moses), and I'm the epitome of this fandom. Nick truly "got" who I was, and instead of fleeing from it, he embraced it.

Before the overwhelming "feels" take control of my tear ducts, I open my mouth to turn off any impending water works. (How dare tears threaten this moment with their sentimental bullshit...) "You aren't going to start airing your grievances yet, right? I'd like to eat something first to build up my strength." I'm trying to think of more jokes to distract me from the tiny fingers of my emotions plucking away at my heartstrings and my eyeballs.

Nick laughs, which is far better music to hear tonight than an out of tune Christmas carol. "Nah, I guess we can wait on that." He stands up and makes his way toward the Festivus pole to retrieve the package resting against it. He straightens and turns himself to face me, pulling me into his captivating gaze — the colored lights on his face more directly accentuating his well-defined features (and dat week-old five o'clock shadow he has going on, yes-yes) — and hands me the package.

"Shalom."

Opening gifts in front of people has always felt really awkward to me. Cards are the worst; you *HAVE* to read it in front of the person and offer some sort of reaction. So, thank God that there doesn't seem to be a card involved right now. I graciously accept Nick's gift, trying to hide my stupid little girl smile under an exaggerated surprised expression, the whole time wondering what he could have possibly done to top the decorated Festivus pole in my living room.

As soon as I tear the last of the brown paper from the package, I lose my shit and laugh uncontrollably.

There in my hands is a custom-made wall calendar. Of sexy Larry David pictures. Let me clarify: Larry David's head is Photoshopped onto "sexy man" bodies. On the front there's a picture of a chiseled, bronzed body framed by an elegant seaside sunset... with Larry David's head pasted on top of the body. My laughter is fueled even more when I realize that Nick probably doesn't have a printer, which means he had to have this printed at a store or some shit. So, someone saw these sexy LD pictures. The only thing that would make the gift any better would be if Nick had taken reaction shots of the clerks while they were printing his order for him and slipped those into the calendar somehow.

I'm finally able to suppress my laughter enough to speak. "Come here, Bubeleh," I tell him as I pull him in to thank him appropriately. I wrap my arms around his neck (Larry gazes upon us in approval from behind Nick's left shoulder) and lay the deepest, most passion kiss I can muster on him. The soft breath from his nose pants lightly against my cheek, and those butterflies start to migrate south. They must be Monarchs.

Our kiss lingers for a moment, and then I gently push away from Nick, remembering the gift bag in my left hand. "Oh! I have something for you, too." I hand the decorative bag over to him.

There is a soft smile on his lips as he accepts the bag and looks inside. He removes its contents, a DVD, and then asks, "*The Room*?" His eyes are curious, and the slight raising of his eyebrow (holy shit, this dude is so freakin' hot) tells me that he has never heard of this cinematic treasure. For those of you less fortunate folk who haven't had the privilege of seeing *The Room*, it's the best and worst romantic comedy ever made. The sincerity of the unrealistic script plus the "flawless" lead actor makes this a must-see for any cinephile.

"As soon as you mentioned that you love *Top Gun* — for all of the right reasons — I knew that you'd love this movie. The fact that you'd never brought up *The Room* told me that you'd never seen it, which needs to change. NOW. It will change your life..." I allow my voice to trail off dramatically. I didn't bother mentioning to Nick that this was my own personal copy of the movie — my favorite movie ever — but he would've given it back to me if he knew. If the wear on the disc is noticeable, he would probably just assume that I'd bought it for a dollar on eBay and not that it was worn from my repetitive viewings of it. The funny thing is that I wasn't sad to give up my most prized possession. As happy as it made me, Nick made me happier.

Turning the DVD over to examine the text on the back, Nick says, "So, how about we eat some artery-clogging food and watch this monumental film to-gether then?"

That's exactly what I wanted to hear. "Sounds good to me. I'll try not to become too distracted by this sexy-as-fuck calendar you got me." I seductively trace Larry's lips with a finger while making the most awkward groaning sound I can muster. How the hell does this guy put up with me?

Laughing, Nick walks over to the "entertainment stand" (an old suitcase that my DVD player sits on) to start the movie. Over his shoulder, he says, "I guess I screwed myself over with that one. You won't give me another look tonight now that you have all of those sexy pictures to look at."

As soon as I'd decided to give Nick *The Room* for Christmas, I knew that I'd locked the doors of Sexy-Time for the evening. The sex scenes in that film could kill the libido of Charlie Sheen. Well, someone might argue that *Top Gun* has the same effect, and look what happened on that blissful evening. The fact that he'd given me my first orgasm was enough to "hold me over" until the mood struck us again, though. Even though I'd love for him to dig into my stocking on this holiday evening, I'm just happy to spend the holiday with the man I love most.

Hey, **Christmas, you're *alright*.**

CHAPTER 21
THE CELLULOID SELF

<u>In the long run, the most unpleasant truth
is a safer companion than a pleasant falsehood.</u>

-Theodore Roosevelt

Every mentally capable individual attempting to understand why he or she deserves to go on taking up space on this ever-shrinking chunk of liquid filled rock stuck in the endless push and pull of the unseen inertia of space is neither a narcissist nor of higher moral standings. Musing on one's own mortality and analytically probing into the unfathomable question: why was I, out of billions of wriggling microscope organisms loaded with potential strands of DNA, allowed to germinate and grow into this spiritually stunted, self-destructive robot that inevitably rusts and becomes obsolete? Finally taking a temporary metaphysical form that shimmers and waivers through infinite worlds unguided, dancing and filling the spaces between threaded dimensions until suddenly disappearing; becoming completely separated from the grand tapestry forever.

The means of turning the organic body into a self-programmed machine of constant consumption and intolerable sensitivities to trivial hardships is something that comes as a second mode of operation for us as Homo Sapiens. Somewhere down our slow genetic timeline, the human brain inadvertently re-wired itself with busted dopamine receptors and diminished frontal lobes that have been wrung dry by popular technology and the lack of real world education.

The second we stop asking ourselves, "Why am I here, and what am I doing to earn my place?" we immediately shut out the possibility of ever truly living life. We mindlessly scroll and sift through other people's digitally projected realities and personas; vicariously existing day to day with only the slightest inkling of what experiencing life feels like without an interactive window to dumbly filter your gaze through. Socially crippling and detrimentally harmful to one's own mental health, this ever-growing trend in human nature is alarmingly dangerous in many ways. Your body runs and moves in the real world while your mind and soul are passively sucked out through rogue waves of shifting, finger sensitive lights; fully integrating to that semi-tangible, alternate state where everyone and everything is just a miniaturized pixel replica serving as a visual testament for man's own slothful avoidance of true enlightenment.

Deaf, blind, and dumb by popular demand, we all stopped asking ourselves the important questions and instead turned our gaze outward towards the hypnotic sparkle and shine of materialistic hedonism. Free thought and unmarketable self-truths are something that used to be a commodity among all right-minded humans, something obtained through weathering years of growth and self-discovery out in the impossibly flawed landscape of true reality. Once our soon to be tangled, hardwired brains figured out that we could boost our own social standings by deteriorating and manipulating countless aspects of everyday existence, we in turn created an ever-expanding gap between the real and the empathetic values that got us to this point of endlessly dwelling in a hyper-state of technological enslavement.

The countless star systems and galaxies, clustered in their deep, seamless pockets of cushy black matter, are always receding and stretching away from one another; becoming gradually colder and more isolated with each passing second. The same can be said of our capacity for existential thought and feelings that evolve beyond one's own petty desires. Thrown under the bus in this act of intellectual sabotage, whether intentional or not I can't say for sure, are the underlying principles of self-worth and more importantly love; the unshakable constant that once thrived in this discarded quasi-human wasteland that now clogs our unusually vast intake ducts. Originally installed for the flow of vital information.

With the time consuming, counter-productive task of manufacturing a celluloid or 3D printed copy of oneself, we all hope and pray that we theoretically live forever in the cloud for future selves to praise and maybe resurrect for another lifetime of continuing the senseless tradition of hopeless narcissism. The only love that can exist in that cold environment is the feverish cultism of neurotic self-worship and false deities.

Suffering the most in this deadly triad of altered images, senseless pandering, and brutally toxic corrosion of moral values is the life altering truth of love. At the risk of sounding like a yoga cult master, I think out of all the philosophical mysteries of the known universe that love is the most important for everyone to firmly understand. It is impossible to fully comprehend love and all its minor offshoots (lust, jealousy, heartbreak) without first knowing its tender kiss and acidic tongue lined with deep cuts that ooze the deceivingly juicy poisons of a tormented heart into your wide, unsuspecting mouth.

To know love is to lose love.

Always progressing through obstacles and loss only to find it once again, even if only for a fleeting moment.

What is said to become of the person who never

experiences these unavoidable trials and tribulations of love? Does this poor, vacant soul simply sit in an emotionally inept purgatory, doomed to spend an eternity standing flatly on his own hands while simultaneously attempting to stand righteous and tall? Does this person toil and crawl through the deep, water logged trenches of life only to get to the end of the line and realize that he somehow got lost somewhere along the way? Answers to these questions are inconsistent due to the fact that no one swims the same trench. The only real, rock solid fact of true love is that a life is not worth living without it.

I fully acknowledge the allure of living vicariously in an existence where immortality and self-hypnosis are readily available to me whenever I feel the need to escape. No matter the time or day, soothing words and pleasant images await me in the ever-growing cybernetic mainframe of the Internet. The idea of dropping my real identity and starting a second life online sometimes seems like the perfect solution to my sorrows. I hear millions of people find love online with dating sites and apps. Sadly, I know it isn't the same. Sure, the new futuristic methods are much more convenient, getting algorithmically matched to a suitor by common interests and preferences, but the process is undeniably flawed. By meticulously framing and categorizing yourself and your expectations of your soon to be "love," you are basically saying that you are so self-absorbed that you could never be with someone who doesn't remind you of you. It's as if everyone forgot that the only way of changing and bettering oneself is to open and expand your identity beyond just physical and trivial interests. By surrounding yourself with carbon copies of You, your chances of ever finding true love or happiness are slim to none. You will be surrounded by nice, friendly faces on the ever-shifting feeds and boards, but you will still be completely empty on the inside; forever starving for real, unconditional affection. I'm not saying that finding love online is impossible; I'm just saying that it is a complete waste of time for someone in my... position. Even with sexy shirtless pics or racy Snapchats, I would only be temporarily sedating the intolerable loneliness that chips away at the rocky surface of my petrified heart with each passing day.

I'd sooner accept death than live in a false reality where superficial replicas of love and hate coexist in long, poorly worded message boards and video comment sections.

I used to feel this weightless absence in my life with every smell, every breath, and every step that I took. Only in the recent months have I found the missing jigsaw piece to the intricate puzzle that validates my existence upon completion. Harper coming into my life at the moment she did was the closest thing to divine intervention that I have ever seen with my own eyes. Just as I was at the point in my life where simply existing day to day with no one to relate and connect to was enough of a reason for me to throw in the towel, she walked into my job and into my heart. A single person can only maintain a healthy demeanor for so long before succumbing to the ego strangling pressure of being unable to escape the label of Unlovable. And while finding love has strengthened my resolution to live, my genetic curse keeps me in a perpetual state of childish flirting and demeaning disseverment from consummating and becoming a true couple.

This pickle of a catch-22 can only stand for so long until the ever-climbing legs get kicked swiftly out from under us. We ascend to the heights of angels while only strengthening our ever-escalating fall into the pitiful depths of Hell. Hell, in this case, being that blank faced purgatory where my head dangles listlessly from my crooked, U-bent spine until I am either moved up the spiritual ladder, or I erode naturally back into the radioactive static of space from which I came.

This suburban journey that we have shared together has been amazing and oddly whimsical. At no point in time during the last six months have I even remotely questioned whether this feeling I have for her is true love or not. Being the sexually experienced Casanova that I am, I chalked up a lot of my feelings at first to simple lust and outright pathetic urgency to find someone, anyone, to be with. Surely one can't blame a tortured soul like me for continuing the stupid tradition of love at first sight. As corny and cliché' as it is, that is exactly what happened. It was as if Harper and I existed apart only to meet later in life when the time was just right. As if our paths were tied together somehow, knotted at one end so our futures merging into one form would be unavoidable.

Too good to be true is one way of describing this whole thing, and I partially agree. While I never questioned our love, I still question the shelf life of said love once Harper finds out that I am a mutant. If my own father, whose defunct testicles spewed the curdled semen that brought me here, can't even love me, then what chance do I have with Harper? She might be too kind to outright hate me for it, but there is no way she simply will not care let alone accept the idea of marrying a human shaped saw horse. I have been sick with worry trying to figure out what step I will take next. While I am sure I could go on eating her snizz and avoiding real sex for a bit longer, I know that eventually she will wonder why I don't want to go to bed with her.

I often wonder if telling another white lie that's a little closer to home would be the best option for prolonging this dream. I could tell her that I'm incontinent or have some kind of sensitivity issue down there, but that would only fly for so long. She would have to see me naked at some point, and with the two fairly large waggle staffs I keep sheathed at all times, I would end up right back where I started; living a shameful life of secrets and deception. I have spent every day for the last six months trying to figure out a way around this, and I have come to one agonizingly painful conclusion.

I have to tell her the truth.

Chapter 22

The Hotdog in the Room

I'll be the first to admit that blizzards scare the shit out of me. This fear is *so* controlling, I check the weather app on my phone every day at the start of the winter season (fall is my start time during those brutally cold years) just to make sure there's nothing ominous waiting for me in the weekly forecast. Some people hold a Christmas countdown. I hold a blizzard watch. Not out of overwhelming excitement, but out of sanity shattering anxiety. Any type of natural disaster gives me unrelenting anxiety, really. Terror moves so rapidly throughout my body that my skin gets feverish. My thoughts become irrational, and I revert to a six-year-old who has watched the *The Thing* for the first time while her parents are out getting drunk at the karaoke bar. It really shouldn't be all that surprising; I'm terrified of pretty much everything.

When I checked the forecast yesterday at the end of work, as is routine, I could feel all my organs pause for a microsecond. There it was: **a warning**. Not an orange advisory or special weather statement. This was a red hang-on-to-your-titties **WARNING**. Had it been a winter storm warning, I would've been frightened, but I would've been able to talk myself down from that ledge of fear. Maybe.

Don't jump; you have so much to live for!

This was a blizzard warning. Yup. **BLIZZARD**. Fuck. Me.

On second thought, maybe you SHOULD jump...

Nick must've sensed my anxiety when I asked him whether he'd heard about the blizzard that was headed our way because he quickly suggested that we spend that night together. He said if the storm became so balls out that we lost power, we could at least keep each other company and throw curses to the wind as a duo.

Thank the heavens that I found such a perceptive gentleman.

What some might call **a nice guy**.

At work, the lights had flickered a warning of what was soon to come. The vacuum in my hand sputtered as the electricity waned in the increasing winds, and I could hear my pulse throbbing in my ears. After this had happened three times, Nick called all of us outstanding citizens together to tell us it was time to call it a night. He didn't want to risk any of us getting into an accident, and he promised he would explain this to Angelica. The others whooped and wailed in triumph at the news (why do people get excited to go home due to bad weather? What the hell are you going to do with your time off???) while I tried to cool the sickness boiling in my stomach — even to a slow simmer would've been nice. I'd only felt sicker when we exited the building. The city had already been butt-fucked by nature. Its splooge had been shot upon everything it could touch.

Fuckfuckfuck—

Come on pussy, keep it together. You've seen snow before. It's not like the world is covered in literal shit.

Well, it might as well be. At least shit is warm.

Before the acid in my stomach had a chance to crawl up my esophagus and leap into the outside world, spewing a colorful array of Easy Mac and diced bananas, Nick turned toward me with those calm eyes, laid a comforting hand on my waist, and said, "The Lumina has studded snow tires. I'll be sure to take it slow. Your apartment is closer, so is it okay if we go there instead of my place?" His cheeks had already developed a warm glow against the biting wind, and his hair was being gradually teased into a slight afro. The winds must've been exceptionally harsh. They had broken through his stubbled cheeks and his God-like, camouflaging skin tone. He looked glorious even during this time of impending doom. I'd almost expected (hoped for) him to tear off his shirt, throw me over his shoulder, and carry me off into the blustering beast of a blizzard. The biting winds would be no match for his erect, pointed nipples.

Before I'd had the chance to fully appreciate this visual, the wind shoved the trees to my right. You know that odd, crackling sound of protest trees make when it's waaaay too fucking cold outside? That weird combination of a creaking and the sound an ice cube makes when you very slowly compress it between your teeth (we all know you've tried it)? Yeah, that sound.

Don't puke.

I smooshed and shit stomped the bad feelings back into hiding where they belonged. "Yeah, my place is fine. Even though its level of crap-titude completely surpasses your apartment, mine has a gas stove, at least. Even the gods of winter won't keep us from enjoying Ramen tonight." I shook a fist toward the sky and flipped it the bird with the other.

Shaking his head at my antics but smiling in spite of himself, Nick passed me his keys. "Why don't you start the car up while I finish locking up? You might want to plug your phone in the charger, just in case we lose power tonight." We both knew that it was a matter of when, not if. It was sweet of him to be optimistic about the **situation**, and I appreciated that.

My cupped hands accepted the keys. "You got it, boss," I said in my best (worst) Georgia accent and stumbled my way to the car, which was surprisingly snow-free. Well, there's one upside to the wind, I guess...

Even with the whine of the engine, I could still hear the wind taunting me. It didn't take long for me to hastily push the volume knob of the CD player on (yes, Nick is a "90's baby" who still listens to CDs — what of it?), missing it completely on the first attempt and stubbing my finger ever so slightly to the side of it (who does that, seriously??), to muffle the shrieks of nature with whatever Nick happened to have listened to on his way to work. My asinine index finger corrected its misstep (it happens, buddy) and pushed down hard to resuscitate the vibrations of sound to drown out reality. Rapturous polyrhythms filled the air around me as *Chaosphere* nut-kicked all sound, and silence, that'd been present inside of the car. Of all times to listen to extreme, Swedish metal... right? But, I could now understand why most metal bands are located in the frostiest climates of the world. This bullshit is totally worth writing angry music about.

At some point, I'd become lost in the atmosphere of the music and almost bailed out of the truck to flee into the night when Nick suddenly jumped into the driver's seat. He was covered in snow and ice, and his snow-fro had frozen in place. If I hadn't been so freaked out by the weather, I probably would've made a joke about his anime inspired do. He calmed the mechanical rhythms to a volume that he could speak over without initiating a shouting contest with the album. "Ready to leave?"

With a double thumbs up, I said, "I was born ready, bruh."

And off we went.

***

Now, here we sit on my curb-abandoned sofa, watching Larry David bitch about a poor park job. Originally Nick had wanted to watch *Fright Night*. My expression must have told him, "You gotta' be outta your fuckin' mind," and he made a new selection. I'd taken it upon myself to make us hot chocolate. I *MIGHT* have neglected to tell Nick that this hot chocolate was spiked with coffee. I knew I wouldn't be sleeping much tonight, and I wanted to better my chances of falling asleep before Nick did. Having built a tolerance to caffeine through my inhuman coffee consumption (thanks, Megan), I knew I'd be much less affected by the stimulant than Nick would be.

Larry is about to explain the dangers of road head, and the electricity vanishes. Gone. Like that. No warnings had been given — not even the slightest flicker. The unannounced darkness takes me by surprise, and I realize that I'm not breathing. Two warm palms guide me sideways, and I feel the familiar warmth of Nick's lips on my forehead. "I'm sorry you didn't get to finish watching *Curb*, Harper, but there's no reason to get upset over it. Do you have any candles or a flashlight that we could use?"

Like any female Caucasian living in America, I

always have at least three scented candles strewn about my living quarters. "Yeah, there's a couple on the kitchen counter, and I think I have one or two in the bathroom. You know how I like my baths in candlelight and my lust for causing fire hazards." I'm doing my best not to sound like I'm going to fill my pants with excrement at any moment. The weight on the couch shifts as Nick (I hope...) leans to grab his phone. I squint as the light from his cell phone penetrates the darkness encasing us. The comfort is immediate as I look into his blue eyes illuminated by the electrified, blue glow spotlighting his face like he's a burlesque dancer taking to the stage. Or, like a groping couple getting the flashlight in a dark movie theatre. Whatever simile you prefer.

"Alright, I'm going to go get those for us. Here's your phone in case you need anything while I'm up." Nick slides my own cell phone into my slightly sweaty hand like a dick into a slick, anxious vagina. I think we both know that the phone is here in case I freak out.

But, you're not going to freak out. You're going to calmly sit here while Nick grabs all your scented candles. It will take him no more than five minutes. Everything is fine.

The couch shifts slightly as Nick gets up. My anchor to rational thought has left me. He's using the cell phone in his hand as a flashlight, but the light is dimmed to conserve battery power. Nick's faintly lit face and hands are all I can see in my dark apartment. I feel almost like I'm in the middle of a videogame as I watch him carefully step around the various obstacles scattered about my floor. He scans the countertop for few seconds before he finds the first candle and lights it. Thank God, I'd carelessly tossed the lighter on the counter. The landlord doesn't care for fire hazards in the home, so I'll usually find a way to hide all my candle paraphernalia. Last night I was anxiously checking my weather app every hour and forgot to cover up my incriminating evidence. For once in my life, my crippling anxieties have paid off. Lifting his head in my direction (I'm not sure whether he can see me or not, but somehow, we still make eye contact), he gives me a thumbs-up before he continues on toward the bathroom.

After Nick rounds the corner toward the bathroom, taking the light with him, I count the reasons why I'm thankful that he offered to stay with me tonight and the infinite reasons why I'm so glad that I found him at this stage of my life. It was only a few months ago that I'd come to the conclusion that I was incapable of truly loving anyone in this damp, disgusting world. Or that I would be able to provide enough emotional satisfaction for someone to want to stay with me. The lethal combination of my eccentric humor and demeanor plus my cynical view of the world had been a recipe for loneliness. Humor helped me to deal with how crushing the world felt to me, but it also caused me to miss out on a very important component to life. Even though my low-brow humor attracted plenty of friendships in my past, it'd alienated me from the dating scene completely. And when I'd entered the dating scene, these qualities of mine were not the most comforting.

In my immature, snarky story, the comedian didn't win love. Yet, here I am on this cliché dark and stormy night with a man who accepts me for what I am. A man who laughs with me and doesn't judge my blunt societal observations. A man who alleviates my irrational fears with an understanding and gentleness. A man who makes this cold, hard world warm and loving. A man whom I so desperately want to **fuck the shit out of.**

Let's be honest, now.

Maybe it will be tonight? You have no power, so there are less activities to keep you occupied this evening. Isn't that what you would see in one of those sappy romantic-comedies, anyway? The power goes out, so the guy and girl do what grown-ups do until morning breaks?

I hadn't watched a lot of romance films — the genre is always so predictable and up its own ass — but it sounded about right. Maybe now's an opportune time to give it another go.

Before I'm able to plan out how to proceed with the evening's sexipades, Nick's back with a candle in one hand and a bundle of what looks like blankets tucked between his arm and side. Carefully, he puts the candle down on the end table (cardboard box...) near my side of the couch. He fills me in on our candle **situation** as he straightens back to a standing position. "I found three candles. There are two in the kitchen, so if you need to find your way to the bathroom, you can grab the extra one. Hopefully the power isn't out for too long so it doesn't get too cold in here. I grabbed a few blankets from your bed, though."

He starts to hand me the bundle.

I have other ideas.

Keeping my eyes on his offering, I count a ten second wait time in my head. I don't want to seem too eager, after all. "Thanks, but maybe we should just go to bed. I mean, there isn't jack-shit to do with the power out, so it seems like we might as well just call it a night, right? It might be easier for us to stay warm using body heat that way." I suck at this. **So hard**.

Ugh, poor word choice...
No, it's the ***perfect*** word choice.

The mass of blankets in his hands hovers for a moment, held out to me like a peace offering, and then retreats back toward his chest. "Yeah, I guess that makes sense. It's getting pretty late, anyway, and I'm starting to get tired."

Hopefully, he isn't too tired.

***

Familiar arms are wrapped around me as I lay here in bed trying to think of the best way to initiate this. I'm not quite sure what is "protocol" for this type of thing (remember how great I am at following those?), and having only seen one romance film in my lifetime that I can remember, I have nothing to reference. Do people talk, or do they just... start?

As gently as I can manage (which isn't so elegant, after all), I roll my body over so that I'm facing Nick, almost head butting him in the nose. *So smooth.* We'd set one of the candles on top of the television screen, so I'm able to see his face softly outlined in its flickering glow. "Thanks for coming over tonight. I probably would've been in the corner shaking and crying by now if I was alone. There might have been poop involved, too."

Really, you're making poop jokes right now?

In the soft light, I can see the signs of a smile on his face. "It's no problem. Might as well be stuck in the dark together than by ourselves, right?"

Before he's able to begin another sentence or I'm able to make some stupid-ass joke, I bring my lips to his. Blindly leaning forward, his lips meet mine. Our hands soon start to wander, gliding gracefully across each other's bumps and curves, mentally tracing outlines of our bodies on the black canvas that fully envelops us. Soon, my hungry hands drift southward, sliding roughly past his loose shirt bottom and plunging into his tight jeans. My fingertips make it through, but the bulk of his belt buckle stops them.

Halt, who goes there!?

Without breaking from the deep kiss, my hands start to work the belt buckle loose as he slides under my bra to gently cradle my tits in his cold, but loving, embrace. Soon, my greedy fingers are fluently unbuttoning the top of his jeans and gently pulling down the heavy metal zipper.

Suddenly, Nick forces my hands away from him, and he pulls himself away from me.

Déjà vu bitch slaps me out of my hot-and-bothered mindset.

"Nick, what's wrong? Did I do something wrong?" I'm really not sure what happened. It seemed like he'd been into what was going on. So, what the fuck? What. The. **Fuck.**

Even in this darkness, I can see that familiar sadness in his eyes. It's the same sadness I saw whimpering behind his eyes on our first night together. He moves to a sitting position, and I follow. "No, you didn't do anything wrong. Harper, we have to talk about something." The discomfort in his voice is infectious. I really have no idea what to expect, and my stomach tries its best to escape this uncomfortable **situation** through my colon.

"If you're worried about conceiving a blizzard baby, don't be. I take birth control pills to muzzle the fury of my monthlies, so we're fine. And if it's STDs you're worried about, that's not a problem. I haven't had sex with anyone since the last time I had an annual check-up. So, my equipment is all clean."

Nick slowly shakes his head. "No, it's nothing like that—"

"Are you not over an ex-girlfriend or something? Am I acceptable to have conversations with, but not sexually attractive to you?" There's an anger building in my voice that I can't suppress. The **situation** is so irritating that I can feel myself becoming irrational. I'm getting tired of this recurring rejection. Typically, it's emotional rejection with a willingness to negotiate friendly fuck sessions. Now, I'm facing sexual rejection, but the dude claims to love me. The fuck is that noise? No. This **situation** is what's irrational — *not* my reaction.

"Harper, it's not you; it's me," Nick says with a sternness in his voice that I've never heard from him before. Somehow, even in this blanket of darkness, I can see the **seriousness** in his eyes.

I can't believe he just used that hackney line on me. It takes everything in me not to begin shredding apart my sheets or hefting miscellaneous objects (the bed, perhaps) across the room. Who does he think he is!? Like I haven't heard this lame-ass line *a million times* in my short lifetime. I can't help but narrow my eyes in a *no you fuckin' **didn't*** glare. It's full Bitch-Mode at this point. "Don't tell me it's not you, it's me. When someone uses that piss-poor excuse, it's the other person 99.9% of the time." I can feel the anger rising like the pressure in a shaken soda can, and I'm not sure how many more drops or prodding I can take before bursting and spewing shrapnel everywhere.

Nick takes one of my hands in his in an attempt to pacify my raging emotions. "No, **seriously** Harper. There's something that I have to tell you. I probably should have told you a while ago, but I didn't think you would stick around, and I didn't want to risk that."

I allow my anger to cool slightly. There's regret amplifying his words. Regret is something I know far too much about. "Okay, so tell me." I cross my arms quickly to make sure he knows that I'm still pissed, though.

There's one of the most uncomfortable pauses I've ever experienced. The silence surrounds us. It's almost as unsettling as the silence that greeted me after I gave my horrible funeral speech. It's thick, unsympathetic, and sadistic. It's almost thick enough to suffocate the howling winds outside which have replaced the ticking of a clock that we so often hear in movies during moments just like this one.

I hear Nick take a slow breath before he tells me, "I have diphallia."

I'd never heard this word before. It sounds scientific and of the medical realm. "Diphallia? What the hell is that? Is it some kind of STD or something?"

"Harper, I have two dicks."

... did he really just say that?

*Wow, you weren't expecting **that**, were you?*

Again, the silence strangles us as I process this information. It's abruptly destroyed by my hysterical laughter. It's uncontrollable and I can't suppress it. The mattress jerks slightly. I guess the sudden break in silence via crazy laughter must've caught Nick off guard. Never has anyone ever tried to use such a bizarre excuse to avoid having sex with me. There was even that one time that a dude told me that he couldn't screw within the first hour after eating. Like it was a fuckin' dip in the family swimming pool. No, this surpasses any excuse that I've ever heard.

I'm finally able to control myself long enough to speak. Nick is staring at me, mouth open in what I assume to be shock. Even if he wants to respond,

I'm not giving him a chance before I spit out what's on my mind. "Am I *that* unappealing to you sexually that you have to make up some crazy shit to avoid having sex with me? I mean, it's been made pretty clear to me on more than one occasion that I'm not fuckable, but **seriously** — this is weak."

Now, the anger has manifested itself in Nick. "Does everything have to be a fucking joke to you!? Why can't you be *serious* for a few minutes?" The words throat-punch me, and I'm unable to speak. It all comes back to this.

You never take life *seriously*.
Girls aren't funny.

Without saying another word, Nick abruptly gets out of bed. The sharp jangle of his keys and the urgent pound of his footsteps are the only sounds in my apartment. He makes his way to the door and slams it shut before I'm able to say or do anything.

I'm left with only the darkness and my own regrets.

Chapter 23
Don't You Eat that Yellow Snow

The only good thing about these short winter days is that the sun isn't here to mock my red, tear-swollen eyes. This is the first time I've walked to work in at least three months, and of course it *has* to be during the darkest month of the year. That's just the way my pathetic existence of a life works. Despite my exhaustion, my legs carry me along without pain or fatigue. Honestly, I feel completely numbed out, almost like I'd been awake for three days straight instead of for a single night. Sorrow takes its toll on a person, I suppose.

The phobia of the dark wasn't even the main instigator of my sleepless night. The majority of the night, in between frantic texts to Nick — begging him to please answer my calls — I'd been doing my best to suck just enough of an Internet connection from the cell phone towers to examine any and every website, science journal, blog, and news article related to the term "diphallia." I would've tried to find YouTube videos, but the Internet connection was too weak to handle that. That may have been a blessing in disguise, in hindsight.

What I'd discovered on the Internet was, at first, a little appalling. I admit it. I learned that it's an incredibly rare condition and every case is different. Of course I, of all people, would fall head-over-tits in love with a guy with "an extremely rare" condition. The results ranged from freakshow to the simply odd. I saw images of body formations that barely resembled a penis (penises?) and others that looked as if El Salvador Dali took it upon himself to add his surreal touches to a portrait of John Holmes. There were science journals documenting that the additional pecker had limited to no function while others showed evidence of two fully functional penises. Basically, it was a crapshoot. Some dudes were pretty lucky. Others were up shit creek.

There was no way of knowing how the dice had rolled for Nick.

*But does it **really** matter? Do you **really** care that much about how many dongs a dude has? You've been seeing this guy for like a half a year, and you've been the happiest you've ever been without sex being involved. What is one extra dick when you are currently getting no dick at all?*

And hey, he's pretty good with his tongue, you know? That's something, right?

Here I am selfishly thinking about how this thing, this **situation** (oh boy, there's that term again...), will affect me when I haven't even thought about how it affects Nick. He's been living with two peckers his entire life. I'd only recently learned that I would indirectly be living with two penises. How did he find out that he was "different" from the other boys? Had anyone known about it? Had some punk kids ridiculed him as a child? Were there any other girls who had found out about his **situation**? How did they react?

My reaction was laughter. What was I thinking?? Instead of taking him **seriously**, I instead personalized the **situation** and made it about me. This isn't about me. This is about Nick. I can't even fathom how my obnoxious reaction had made him feel. I'm a poor excuse for a human being who doesn't deserve to breathe, let alone drink gourmet coffee on a regular basis.

And then there are the questions about sex. Given his **situation**, is Nick a virgin? Is he even able to get it (them, I guess) up? I'd had the opportunity to briefly fondle at least one of the Johnson twins, so I think it's safe to assume that at least one has *some* functionality based on the warmth and fullness I was able to palm. The girth of it was pretty impressive, more than a handful, so one erection is possible. I also think it's safe to assume that, perhaps, he has even less sexual experience than I have.

Which is phenomenally little.

The truth of the matter is I've had a very limited sex life up to this point. Nick is the best thing to happen to me, really. After all the shit that'd happened with Will, I thought I'd never be in another relationship again because of the overwhelming guilt. Guilt that I wasn't a good person, let alone a good girlfriend. Guilt that I'd let down a person I cared about. Somehow, Nick was able to help me forget about that guilt.

Okay, so maybe I didn't *forget* about the guilt completely, but it's easier for me to accept that there really was nothing I could've done in that **situation**. Will's struggles with mental health were happening long before we'd become an item. There were endless changes in prescriptions. He kept his inner turmoil hidden from the world around him and instead numbed it out with the most natural anesthetic out there: humor. I guess I was sort of like his drug dealer, in a way. But, who's to say whether his life would've been better or worse without me around? Since I've been with Nick, I've been able to gradually cope with the tragedy and have come to accept the reality of what had happened. Will had lost the struggle, and he was too far gone to come back from this loss. Nick had also helped me to accept the idea that maybe, just *maybe*, I am loveable.

But, does he still love me?
Did I lose my chance with **a nice guy**?

A jolt surges through my limbs as the obnoxious drone of a car horn breaks my thoughts. A red rust bucket of a Dodge Neon (oohh, but check out them rims — they're real puss magnets) swerves sharply around me (***ON THE CROSSWALK***) as the driver continues to lean on the horn. Instinctively, I flick off the driver and invite him/her to, "Suck my dick," as he/she speeds off into the dark of the night.

Nice word choice, there...

Fuck you. I used the singular noun.

Now that I'm shaken from my fogged thoughts, I see the flashing, neon yellow lights of *Dandy Don's Dodge Dealership* just a couple of blocks away. My stomach tightens in an excrement-anticipating spasm. It isn't that the douche bag in the Dodge shook me up so much that I now have a resentment for any vehicle of that type, or even the offensively tacky placement of the pink, smiling car on the sign. This is tonight's cleaning location. In only a matter of minutes, I'll have to face Nick. I want to apologize to him about what had happened the night before, but I have no clue where to begin. This is something totally out of my comfort zone. Not only will I have to talk about my feelings without cracking some stupid fucking joke to alleviate my discomfort, but I'll have to talk about a topic the majority of human beings have never even had to *think* about. It's going to be hard as hell, but I have to do it — even if the unease of the **situation** makes me blow chunks all over myself.

You work for a cleaning service. There will be chemicals and the equipment needed for cleaning up puke.

With this encouraging thought, I take a slow, icy breath and begin to move my feet.

***

"What do you mean, he called out??" I'd thought it was weird that I didn't see Nick's car waiting outside of *Dandy Don's* parking lot. At first, I'd just assumed that he was running behind because he was dreading seeing me. I get that. After I asked Bobby if he knew what time Nick was going to show up, the answer had caught me by complete surprise. Nick never called out. Angelica had to force the guy to use his vacation time for Christ's sake.

Bobby looks at me with his sleepy, sunken eyes. "Yeah, he called out fur tha' week. Angelica din' say why, and Nick din' when he called ta tell me dat' I needed to grab tha' supplies this week." The glass coating on Bobby's eyes tells me that he's high as usual, but no higher than what was the Bobby norm. He isn't trying to lie to me (I don't even think he's smart enough to lie), and he hadn't misinterpreted the messages.

Nick isn't coming.

Frantically, I fish my cell phone out of my pocket and send five rapid-fire texts to Nick.

> **Where are you?**
> **When can I see you??**
> **I really need to talk to you, please**
> **I love you.**
> **I need you.**

It's after the inward-farting sound of the final sent text that Bobby starts to speak (mumble) again. "Harper, ken' I be real witchu' for'a secon?" His slouched shoulders had at some point turned to face me instead of what I was used to: him turned slightly to the side as if he always had better shit to do.

Deciding against my better judgment, which is to crack a joke about the aptitude of Bobby's "realness," I put my phone away with shaking hands. I press them both deep into my coat pockets to try to calm the shakes as best as I can. "Yeah, sure Bobby. What's up?" I try my best to hide how much I'm screaming inside.

Bobby keeps his hands in his pockets, too — it was more like his fingertips because his pants clung to his upper thighs — as he speaks and constantly shifts his gaze awkwardly. "Tell ya tha' trooff, I'ma little worried 'bout Nick. He's tha' type'a dude who never calls out. Last time he called out was cuz he had crazy-bad shits, and it was phiskly impossible fo' him ta be here. Jus... seems weird, s'all." His sleepy gaze sets upon something, real or imaginary, off to his right. This is a side of Bobby I've never witnessed before. He's showing concern for another human being, and he's focused on something other than himself and all of his "gangster" coolness for once. Hidden deep within that gunky crust of a man is a person capable of sympathy.

No shit.

My fingers dig into my hair, hardly noticing that the hand has escaped from its temporary prison.

"Yeah, I know. It's really weird, and I was expecting him to be here..." The world around me starts to become caught in the whirling thoughts in my head as I try to determine my next steps. Everything spins around me. I feel like I'm going to hurl. My heart tightens and stops.

Bobby sluggishly shifts his gaze from whatever he was looking at to me. We lock eyes for a moment in silence.

The answer is clear.

"Bobby, I have to go." I start zipping up my coat before my sentence is finished.

Bobby nods at me in mutual understanding. "No prob. I'll keep thins in check, here. Tha' girls n' me got this." Quickly, he does the Bobby Shuffle to the vacuum cleaner. He wheels it down the hall to avoid more *Real Talk* and so he can get a head start on the long night ahead of him y las chicas. I want to thank him for his compassion and understanding, but he's gone before I have the chance.

I abandon *Dandy Don's* with a too forceful push into the front door that almost knocks me on my ass. At first, I think the whiteness showering down on me is my vision preparing my body to faint as a way of avoiding a **serious** conversation. I figure out that the reality is almost as terrible. The snow has started again. This wasn't just the aftershock flurries that sometimes fart out of the snow clouds after a blizzard. These were thick, heavy globs of cold death. My heart gains about five pounds when my fumbling fingers realize that my designated headphone pocket is empty. I must've forgotten them on my way out today because of how tied up in my thoughts I'd been.

Not good.

You've got to be fucking kidding me...

Instead of whining like a little bitch about my **situation**, I tie my hood on tight — the strings hissing — and play "Don't Eat the Yellow Snow" and "Nanook Rubs It" on repeat in my head.

CHAPTER 24
<u>YOU ARE WHAT YOU IS</u>

Alone, I sit slumped against the cold stucco wall that borders the right side of my bed. The faint whispers of distant snow plows and slow-moving traffic on some adjacent street somewhere off in the frozen tundra that used to be a sunny seaside city barely reach me in my current semi-catatonic state. The whirring and hissing of the snow driven wind bleeds effortlessly through the brittle, frost lined windows that serve as the only source of light in this now shadow stained apartment. Sitting here in the dark with nothing but my thoughts and the faint pitter-patter of the other building tenants somewhere unseen, I breathe harsh, damp breathes through spongy, collapsible lungs as my mind grinds endlessly with self-ridicule over the events that led me to this moment.

Head in my hands and knees pulled up to my chest, I breathe deeply through my stiff, knitted fingers as every muscle in my body quivers in anticipation for what is to come. I had not planned on doing this so soon, but the very idea of seeing her at work or by accident on the street makes me physically ill. By all accounts, I think I hung around longer than most people in my position would have, and now I say enough is enough.

Suicide is the only feasible option I have left.

Honestly, this isn't the first time that the idea has popped into my head. I actually used to fantasize about it a lot. Not because I have some sick fascination with death, but because I could never quite accept who or what I was. Coming to terms with the very real idea that you will probably die alone and utterly unappreciated is just as much terrifying as it is demoralizing. You can't honestly expect the guy born with no muscle control in his face to literally put on a smile and stop being such a downer, can you? Do you tell the little girl born with no arms to pick herself up and stop being such a Negative Nelly?

The very notion that there is someone for everyone out there in this great, big, wide world with a population in the trillions only makes me feel smaller and more insignificant. If Harper can't be the girl that I end up spending the rest of my assumably mundane life with, then I say that it is completely within my own right to step out boldly into that blank open space and begin the rolling eons of quiet unknowing. By hanging around and subjecting everyone to my crybaby antics and miserable view-points, I am only going to infect other happy, normal people who don't radiate negativity and display signs of an obvious ego-deficiency.

My strong sense of resolution to be a man and own up to the truth failed me miserably. I thought I could deal with telling her the truth, but when she broke out into girlish fits of laughter over the news of my broken pitchfork, I practically had an aneurysm right then and there. I can see the humor in it, sure. Getting rejected takes many forms; outright glee at someone else's debilitating birth defect is definitely one of them.

Only now can I see that my love life is a Möbius strip of horrible dates and bad decisions; one long string of events that appears to curve into a new, entirely different position only to find that you never really switched sides. Knowing this now, stuck in an endless loop of false turns and spins, there is no way I can see the point in continuing to live.

The stick is ever present, but the carrot is rotten and crawling with nasty, bow-legged insects. It is time to toss the carrot and break the stick.

I never could decide which method of execution would best suit me. My resources are limited, and I never really considered it seriously up until now. With few options to choose from, I mentally scroll my list.

Option #1: *Death by Bullet*

The idea of somehow botching a suicide and being revived, possibly living my life out as a brain-dead vegetable in some sterile hospital somewhere, is an all too real possibility for me and must be avoided at all costs. That's why taking a shotgun or even a measly .22 peashooter to the skull is almost always the quickest, and supposedly painless, means of escape around. The doctors or paramedics aren't going to scrape your brains off the back wall and staple you back together again like some kind of grotesque hamburger Humpty Dumpty. Once most of your skull is flapped open like a rusty old kennel door, then commonly the humane thing to do is to let it rest. Unfortunately, acquiring a gun would mean coming up with some money — fast. I currently have about $50 in my bank account, and unless Walmart is having a firearms and ammunition blow out sale that I am not aware of, that leaves me stranded in a brewing shit storm with no umbrella. I simply just can't hold out that long. So as much as I would like to pull a Hemingway, big toe looped in heavy, spring-loaded steel, I must regretfully choose another mode.

Option #2: *Death by Blade*

While not as fast or as efficient as a gun, cutting one's wrist or jugular is a fairly quick way to cross the threshold of existence. Slitting both my wrists in the bathtub would be my best bet with Option #2, maybe cutting off my main vein(s) to further quicken the process along. The symbolism wouldn't be lost on the poor paramedic who finds my bloated corpse weeks later. Having the means to carry this out, I wonder how long it would take, and I eventually toss the idea aside. I want my suicide to be either quick or painless. Option #2 offers me none of these, so we push forward.

Option #3: *Death by Electrocution*

Another one involving the use of my bathtub. I might cause a power outage or some damage to the apartment interior with this plan, so I think I will skip it. Just because I am going to kill myself doesn't mean I am going to go out like a jerk and inconvenience others any more than I already have. I would hate to be the cause of an electrical fire that wiped out the whole building and put dozens of people out in the streets with nowhere to go. There has to be a poisoned porridge that is not too hot but not too cold for my delicate situation. I want to draw as little attention to myself as possible, so killing myself in the apartment is off limits. Moving on.

Option #4: *Death by Drugs*

Probably the most logical option (of course) on the entire list, death by drugs is something that can be achieved by most people with relative ease. Hell, there are thousands of people every day who accidentally overdose on prescription pills, so they must be good for something. With hours until the pharmacy and liquor stores close, I am a mere two block stroll from acquiring all the things I need. A jar of high dosage sleeping pills and a bottle of cheap vodka would be more than enough to liquefy my aching soul clear through my hard, vein-riddled shell.

As insurance, I think I will carry this out down by the shore as to avoid any interruptions that might interfere with my hasty metaphysical jump. With the beaches closed and the sand blanketed with ice and snow, I am sure to find an isolated spot without issue. If I get really lucky, high tide will creep up the beach and come find me in the night, sweeping my stiff, frozen corpse clean to the ocean floor where no one but hungry plankton and algae will find it. I would like it very much if my body was never found to save my mom the heartbreak and expense of organizing my funeral, but I can't possibly prepare for every detail with such little foresight. If I am found before the shifting sea can pull me back to the birthplace of our species, then oh well. I highly doubt Harper will care much that I am gone now, anyway. I thought about mailing her a note explaining that I had to move across the country to find myself or something gay like that and how none of this was her fault, but what would be the point? She would surely laugh her ass off at that, too, and toss the note into the trash along with the all-pleasant memories that we have shared over the past blissful months together.

If I am going to do this, then I have to act now before I either change my mind and chicken out, or someone like Harper or my mom gets a hold of me, weakening the already crumbling wall that borders the tiny, sun scorched field in my mind where hope and foolish longing still lazily play.

Quickly, I leap up from my bed and grab my jacket and keys off the magazine littered kitchen counter and trudge silently for the door. I take one last look back at the small, poorly furnished room before sliding on my coat and turning to leave. As I unlatch the deadbolt and pull open the door, I am forced to stop dead in my tracks. A tiny figure is silhouetted in the dim orange glow of the single hallway light. Its dark hourglass shape and crimson halo stand boldly against the onslaught of warm orange light emanating from just beyond its statuesque pose.

Not expecting someone at my door, I panic a little, trying desperately to adjust my eyes to the onslaught of light bathing the side of me that isn't still enveloped in the sticky darkness of my recently vacated apartment. I stood in the open doorway, a statue frozen in the middle of the splintered, colorless frame, heart pounding and twisting in my chest like a caged baboon. Suddenly, the blurry figure comes into focus, and my heart does a series of spastic twitches that make me feel as if I might be having a stroke.

There standing in front of me in the dust clogged, shadow lined hallway is Harper. Her hair is noticeably damp and stiff from the snow, and the realization hits me that she must have walked across town in the ever-evolving frozen wasteland outside. Her intense fear of night is bagged under her eyes and unfolding in the creases of her slightly chapped mouth. I never let on to Harper that I knew of her fears to shield her from any embarrassment, but the signs had always been there. How did she manage to walk all this way in the dark, let alone in the middle of a snowstorm? Like some corny *Lifetime Channel* drama where the typical gender roles are reversed, Harper battled her deepest fears just to see me. I stare blankly into her puffy, emerald eyes until her tiny, timid voice breaks through the thick cloud of awkward tension.

"Hi, Nick. Can we talk for a second?"

I should've known this was going to happen. Even when I am trying to do what is right, the random, malicious forces at work sense this and drive a wedge right down the middle of my plans for a permanent vacation. I can't let her apologize and ask to remain friends. I would almost surely say yes and then spend the next countless years watching the only woman I ever truly loved slowly drift and fade into the unretractable depths of the *Friend Zone*. I can't go back to those days where we talked and laughed all night at Bobby and his shitty antics without feeling that twinge of blissful divinity that she makes me feel whenever we are together. I could just as soon do that than move on and find another beautiful girl who is as perfect and as original as Harper.

My brain kicks me in the back of the teeth and forces me to respond after several agonizingly stagnant moments of hanging silence.

"I... was just leaving, actually," I say robotically, dropping my eyes to the ground as I move out of the doorway and make to close the door behind me. As I half turn to make sure the door latches, Harper lunges at me and buries herself deeply into the front of my jacket, hands clenching desperately at my sleeves.

"I'm so sorry! I didn't mean to hurt you, Nick. That's the last thing I'd ever want to do. I honestly thought you were fucking with me at first. Can we please go inside and just talk for a little bit? I promise I won't be long."

I am not looking at her, but I can feel the invisible pull of her gaze turned up to my wondering, stoic steel eyes. Her cheeks undoubtedly streaked with tears and trembling in resistance to the flood welling up behind her eyes. I fight the urge to gaze into them until her hands drift to my face and force me to look down at her.

Our eyes explode in a sudden reaction of kinetic energy. Her down turned lips and sorrowful expression fill me with a sadness so deep that I almost melt in her chilly, outstretched hands. With pressure building behind my eyes now, I stare deeply into her pleading, pain stricken face, overwhelmed with perplexed feelings of love and hate.

"I love you, Nick," Harper finally sobs into my chest in big, whooping gasps. Her warm tears roll down the waterproof lining of my jacket. "You're the only person who has ever made me feel special and needed. When I'm not with you, I just think about how much I miss you and when I'll be able to see you again. No other person has made me feel like I mattered. Even when I first met you, I knew that you were special, and I loved you. You had me at Zappa, Nick."

Fresh tears trail sooty lines across her hot cheeks. She looks up at me with wide, swimming eyes full of helpless anguish. "If you're still too pissed off to forgive me I get that, but it really freaked me out that you didn't show up for work and that you ignored all of my texts and calls. I thought..." I watch her eyes simmer with thought, and I can tell that she is wrestling with some internal conflict unknown to me. Harper squeezes her eyes closed for a few moments before opening them and continuing on.

"Nick, before I moved here, I didn't have much luck in the love department. I had some decent friends, but no one ever looked at me in a romantic way. I was always a joke, and I just sort of went with it. I ended up dating a friend of mine by default. Right before I moved here, he killed himself. I hadn't bothered to pick up on the warning signs, and I wasn't able to help him. I felt like it was my fault he died — like I'd been a shitty girlfriend and friend, and that I let him die. All of the people back home seemed to feel that way. So, I moved here.

"At first, it seemed like a stupid decision. I knew nothing about South Harbor. I had no money. I had no job. Hell, I'm afraid of the fuckin' dark and had to spend every night alone in a sort-of city. I felt lost — I felt defeated..."

Harper pauses for a moment. As she lifts one of her delicate hands, I expect it to move to the back of her head as it usually did any time she started to become uncomfortable. Instead, she uses it to retrieve one of my own hands.

"Then I met you, Nick. I knew from the first day I met you that there was something special about you. At first I thought, 'Oh, this guy is pretty cute,' and once we started to talk in that poopy bathroom, I felt like I was in some sappy dream written by Nicholas Sparks. You were too perfect, and I wanted you to be mine right then.

"Now, I have to live with the fact that I've hurt the person who has made me the happiest I've ever been. I've already failed one person, and I don't want to repeat the same mistake. I love you, Nick, and I'm so sorry."

She trailed off into another burst of tears, holding me tighter with every gasp and sniffle against my chest. There is time to gently pry her from me and just walk away, but I know I can't do it. My love for her is so great that I would rather live a thousand years as a sexless freak than die knowing that I was responsible for ruining her life. Having this happen to her for a second time would surely destroy her physically as well as spiritually.

"Harper," I begin to say shakily, "I can't keep going on like this. I love you more than anything, but I don't think I can handle us just being close friends. Things have progressed too far for that now, and I don't want to keep having to lie to you."

Taking my hands from my sides and placing them gently on her slim shoulders I say, "I'm sorry, Harper. I have to go now," and attempt to lightly guide her away from me. She feels my push and heavily moves a couple inches back before halting and grabbing me firmly by the face again. With her hands clasped around my cheeks, she stares into my soul and speaks the most important words that I would ever hear in my life.

"Who the fuck said anything about just being friends? I love you, Nick, and I want you right now." She then plunges her lips onto mine and takes me back to that place of endless clangy wind chimes and stirring summer winds. A time when everything was right in the world and nothing would ever be otherwise. Our highly charged embrace lasts minutes until I finally force myself to ask the obvious.

"So... does this mean you are okay with my... um..." I stammer to find a professional name to call them. As shallow as it is, I know the relationship will never work if there is no sexual chemistry between us, and I have to know if she is really going to accept me for the whole package or not. A strictly platonic relationship wouldn't be awful, but it is definitely a long way from ideal. Her face draws back from mine. For a second, she simply stares introspectively into my eyes.

"Nick," she starts to say, fingers now delicately unzipping the front of my jacket, silently tracing the hidden lines of my abdomen under my shirt with the smooth palm of her hand, "you could have three scrotums and seven assholes for all I care. I just want to make this thing between us work. If we can't, then at least we can say we tried, right?" She waits eagerly for a response.

I stand in front of her, tears now swelling in my eyes, and am at a loss for words. This is the moment where I either recede back into the shallow pools of my self-conscious egotisms, or I lay everything on the line and put our love to the ultimate test. A decision has to be made, and it has to be made now.

Without a word, I take Harper's hand into mine and guide her quietly into the black void just beyond my open apartment door.

Chapter 25
Love's Inertia

Nick leads Harper through the creaking doorway of the shapeless apartment and then turns momentarily to reflexively shut and lock the heavy wooden door. He turns back to face the outlined figure that lovingly outstretches from his twitching, sweat-laced hands.

"Are you sure you want to do this?" Nick asks, clearly nervous, but still hopeful.

Harper says nothing. Instead, she closes the gap between them and again finds his eager lips and tongue waiting for her touch. His hands soon find her curvy hips, pulling them into his until they are both locked together in a fiery embrace. The kiss breaks mutually as they blindly explore each other's bodies in the velvety blackness of the lightless room.

The sexual tension is almost unbearable. Even in the pitch-black night, they could see the fire burning behind each other's eyes, neither of them having the guts to make the first crucial move. This meeting had been a long time coming, and now that they were here, neither of them knows how to proceed. It isn't until he leans over and gently kisses the shallow dip of her neck that the awkward tension finally leaves the room.

"Oh, God... please don't stop," Harper begs as Nick's hard, calloused fingertips run the curves of her lower back under her shirt. His hot, damp breaths roll down her spine, causing her skin to break out in goose pimples. The feeling of his rough unshaven cheeks rubbing against her makes her skin lightly blush all over — her body to pucker and wilt like some exotic flower freshly picked out of the deepest and most forbidden Amazonian jungle.

With that last kiss, their bodies go into a primitive dance, undressing and passionately kissing in the dark, all the while moving towards the bed.

They were now one entity, sharing one pulse, one mind melded in the moment of this undeniable wanting to touch souls, even if only for a microsecond.

Landing roughly on the piles of sheets and laundry that clutter his bed, Nick forcibly breaks from the deep kiss to say, "I've never done... I mean, this is the first time I..." He then feels a light, night painted finger line his lips, an all too familiar sign from Harper, and immediately understands that she knows that he is a virgin. Her lack of a response tells him that the fact was mute, and nothing has changed since admitting it. With that, he gently rolls her onto her back and slides to the foot of the bed. With her legs spread open, he proceeds to kiss down her silky inner right thigh until she can only make out his crown of curly blonde hair.

Waves of ecstasy roll through her like the mighty tide of a dark moonlit ocean. With each nibble or kiss from his slippery, wet mouth comes a spastic electric charge that courses up and down her spinal cord, numbing her appendages. When it is time to switch, she feebly picks herself up and embraces him with much surprise to his eagerness to receive. Like her, his body is tight with the mirrored feelings of intense pleasure and wavering restraint. The worries of how she would react to his package are soon forgotten once he feels her tight fingers anxiously gripping and pumping both shafts.

Soon her moist mouth is on him, sucking and licking, only stopping to switch hands and to give the other thick, swelling member the same lustful attention. With surprising skill, she juggled both with an eager zeal that simultaneously surprised and scared Nick. If she kept up this ever-quickening pace with her skillful tongue, he would surely blow before they even had a chance to formally meet. He runs his fingers lightly through her hair and stops her just long enough to steal another kiss, hoping to bide himself some time to further build up his almost non-existent sexual stamina.

When she senses her turn is over, they both embrace in a lover's kiss and fall to the bed.

"This is all I ever wanted," she breathes, her voice barely above a whisper. A single tear tumbles down her rosy, warm cheek. He leans in and kisses her lips softly in response, then cautiously tries to enter her with the reproach of a true gentleman. With lefty up to bat, Nick pokes and prods Harper blindly until she graciously reaches down and guides him to her impossibly tight, but anxiously slippery, hole.

Immediately upon entrance, she begins to grab at the sheets with clenched fists, her eyes rolling around widely as if the very room around her were spinning like a top. He can tell that his size did not disappoint her and decides to glide in a little farther now, letting her warm essence envelope him fully. Soon, his hips start to sway in a pendulous rhythm that only gets stronger and faster with each passing thrust. The tool not being used dangles passively off to the side, bobbing and sometimes slapping against their sweat-greased thighs when the thrusts become progressively stronger and deeper. With a free hand, Harper sporadically reaches down to stroke and polish the patient one while he silently waits for his turn to ride.

Surprisingly, Nick's sexual anxieties and fears are muddled under the sweet sounds of heavy breathing and euphonious skin-to-skin contact. Every tendon and muscle in his body has temporarily taken control of his main motor functions and thoughts. For the first time in his life, he is truly living in the moment. His brain is nothing more than a reflective slab of neurons and tissue, absorbing every push and touch with unguarded openness. This convenient short-circuiting allows him to quicken his pace without fear of prematurely reaching the apex.

Harper has no choice but to scream in utter joy while Nick's hands work her sensitive nipples into little pink diamonds. Soon his mouth is upon them, teeth biting and tongue lapping, all the while maintaining a steady rhythm and even flow with his hips. As if on autopilot, he momentarily leaves her breast to once again scoop her up in his strong arms and slide her to the corner of the bed. Completely dazed at this point, she lays stunned while he gently parts her thighs and re-enters her with the other tool, using a little less caution than before.

With the angle changed, his girth enters her with much more impact, causing her to screech in pain and excitement. He pauses momentarily at this. Once no objection has been made, he proceeds. Once again his hips gyrate into motion, and soon she too is swaying and pushing to the beat of their wordless song. Steam rises from their sweaty, naked bodies as the strenuous pull of love's inertia sweeps them along on a blind wing to the internal decadency of true spiritual alignment. With him fully in her and she fully receiving him, the lines of their identity blur like fresh tears rolling down the page of a beautiful poem.

At this moment, Harper has all but forgotten about the brewing storm just outside those thin, frosted windows. Just like Nick, she is lost in the whirlwind of once thought to be unattainable lust and euphoria. Her eyes roll heavenward, as if trying stubbornly to see the fireworks popping and sizzling just behind her numb, O-shaped face. Every lobe inside of her head oozes and shivers with neurotic ecstasy as waves of unseen bliss pour down upon them from forces unknown.

With her arms wrapped around his torso, she eagerly pulls him into her. Sweat rains down from his thriving body like a freak summer storm. The pace quickens, meanwhile, both parties simultaneously keeping time with their metaphysical metronomes, their pounding flesh reverberating off of these sterile white walls that cease to confine them emotionally.

They are both nearing the end now. She senses this the most by his hardness and he by her tightness, but in reality, all logical thought is abandoned to make space for the hot passion that raged inside of them, yearning to be set free.

The bubbly, tingly feeling is rising. Every neuron and particle inside of them is shivering and with only several more strokes, they would climax in a chorus of guttural grunts and jaw clenched hisses. Just when they both think that the pressure building up inside of them couldn't get any more intense, the world suddenly floods with blinding, white fire that incinerates every piece of matter in existence but them. Roaring stars and galaxies rush past them as they gaze intensely into each other's eyes at the exact moment of the nerve shattering shared orgasm. Acting totally on intuition, Nick pulls out just as he is cumming and angles both hoses directly at Harper's midsection. White streams of hot, sticky semen jet out from him and pummel her senselessly while she writhes on the wrinkled sheets. Covering her in his liquid essence, Harper moans savagely, sensually rubbing the pooling white globs into her breasts and stomach, savoring the warm slickness of his fresh seed.

Once all matter bleeds back into focus and the pounding pulse in their ears dissipated, Nick leaves Harper's side to get her a clean towel and a bottle of water from the fridge. Saying nothing, she graciously accepts these gifts and then pulls Nick back into bed.

Chapter 26

THE GIRL IN THE MAGNESIUM DRESS;

Po-Jama People

Staring vacantly at the depthless, ever receding blackness of the ceiling hanging above his head, Nick firmly cradles Harper's sweat covered body in the crotch of his right arm, holding her close to his chest, their heartbeats softly thumping ancient secrets to each other in Morse code. Both feeling completely drained of every ounce of precious liquid that once surged aimlessly through their now naked, tender bodies, they both become deathly silent, mentally preserving the pureness of the moment. The bitter cold from outside leaks in through the many cracks and holes in Nick's low rent apartment. That sneaky bastard Jack Frost tickling and pinching at their damp, exposed skin as they lay open and vulnerable to his unwelcome touch. See-ing Harper's curvy frame start to shiver, Nick leans forward and pulls the blanket up from the foot of the now disheveled bed.

As their motionless bodies sink into the quick-sand of deep, physically regenerating sleep, Nick could vaguely make out something in the approach-ing veil of swirling darkness. His brain, now nearly halfway through its integration from conscious to unconscious, is beginning to lag. The blurry image growing in his sights is something crude and shape-less, but emits a familiar, hollow dullness that tugs and prods at his scattered memory banks. Then, just as he is about to naturally slip through the thin membrane lining that separates fantastic untold fan-tasies from the rough stone altars of unrelenting re-ality, the answer came to him.

The void.

A crisp, tender breeze carries along the scents and soul of the passing winter solace, making way for spring. Its mild coolness is not uncomfortable, but rather consoling and almost warming in antic-ipation of the season of renewal to calmly take the throne as Winter takes her rest. It is time for blos-soming, longer days. It is time for change. The budding limbs of the trees brighten the already ra-diant day, accenting the hues of oranges and reds as the sun sinks beneath the horizon. The clouds blush as the sun slips into the tree line. The waves softly serenade the world, coaxing it to succumb to the serenity of the moment. Carrying it to slumber.

Nick is gazing into the empty, dissonant void that had enveloped him for countless dreams and nightmares over the past seventeen years of his life. Waves of negative electromagnetic impulses crash and ricochet all around him, but he feels none of the usual blinding effects from this direct exposure. Scanning the corner-less space that fills his lidless eyes, Nick has another sudden flickering instant of vivid self-awareness before sleep has a chance to completely encase his entire being. What he realizes is that he is not simply in the void; he is of the void. This polarizing shift in consciousness finds him now standing in a luminescent sea. Glittery pink bands of razor edged light effortlessly carve and slice through the immeasurable, featureless chasm of dead ions and thick, carbonless fog before him.

Nick sits with Harper, his arm resting on the bench behind her. In the receding chill, his warmth delicately kisses her neck and shoulders. The drifting clouds reflect off his blue-gray eyes like falling rose petals. How long they have been sitting here together remains a mystery to her. Harper feels as if she could remain in this moment for eternity. There are no other bodies, no obligations, no uncertainties. There is only Them.

No longer does he blindly sift and crawl through miscellaneous heaps of decayed and rotting memories.

No longer do those columns of misty, spinning windows loom over him as he scratches and slithers his way through that perilous groove that buffers between dimensions yet conceived. Nick has finally ascended to those towering columns. What he once believed to be false alternate realities, against all odds, turned into living prophecy. He now permanently occupies those translucent, plasmid windows, leaving his dream girl only momentarily to peer out into the void. Reminding himself of how lucky he is to be free. A once desperate, insecure fool who was brought to life by the awe inspiring inner beauty and unwavering acceptance of his one true love.

Turning to face Harper, Nick's prominent nose casts a slight shadow down his cheek as the sun says his final farewell. With the gentleness of the most skilled Yogi, Nick collects and then cradles Harper's hands in his own. His eyes never leave her. As the sun finally flickers out of existence, Nick says, "Harper, I need to tell you something."

His metamorphosis into a real man is now complete.

The sounds of the waves begin to fade as if manipulated by a volume knob. Nick has Harper's full attention. She awaits his statement. The tempo of her heartbeat almost overpowers all other sounds. All other thoughts. Those blue eyes glance downward at their clasped hands for a moment. They return to their gaze into Harper's.

Unconsciously, he has obtained what once seemed alien, and uncertain even, in dreams and in waking life. He had finally found the long missing piece to the crude jigsaw puzzle that formed his life. He had finally found his way out of the bottomless pit of tireless souls blindly reaching out with phantom limbs, in hopes of clearing the mist and climbing those towering, twirling lights and oddly fluxing portals to futures unknown.

Nick plucks a beautifully forked flower that has somehow managed to prosper after such a long winter. He delicately lays this in Harper's hands. He whispers, "I love you."

He had finally found the heart of the hydra.